Claimed Bride

The Bride Series

Book 1

By

Linzi Basset

Linzi Basset

Claimed Bride

Copyright © 2018 Linzi Basset
Edited: Anumeha Gokhale
Proofreaders: Marie Vyer, Melanie Marnell
Published & Cover Design by: Linzi Basset
ISBN: 13: 978-1724380128

Linzi Basset

Claimed Bride

Contents

Linzi Basset

Claimed Bride

Author's Note

Dear Reader,

The Bride series are the stories of gorgeous and successful Alpha Males and the sassy women they choose as brides. Although some characters will appear in other books in the series, all of them are standalone novels.

In *Claimed Bride, Book 1*, we meet billionaire Alexander Sinclair who might have done the wrong thing to claim the delectable Penelope Winters as his bride.

Penelope was not having a good week.

First her newly minted 'Ex'husband (*she was going to get a t-shirt made*) decided to drive off into the sunset (literally) and left her in a pile of shit (figuratively). She'd barely put some dirt on it (*actually*), when the most gorgeous man on planet Earth showed up and opened his stupid mouth. Alexander Sinclair—billionaire extraordinaire, real estate mogul, one part of Rogues of Manhattan trio, and all parts wrong for her!

"I need a wife . . . and I don't do pretend, Penelope."

Alex was not having a good week (either).

First, his star employee took millions of investors' money to his grave, leaving Alex to deal with a bloody mess. It got worse (*liar!*) when he went hunting for the wicked Mrs. Carver, but found a delicious little fire-cracker instead. Alex took one look at Penny and bid adieu to his brain (*the one in his head at any rate!*). How else could he explain his insane attraction for this sinfully-sexy-potentially-deceptive-caveman-invoking woman?

Sparks fly as the Penny and Alex clash in a battle of wills . . . and tangle of limbs (*you'll see*). But the Houdini embezzler is still at large and Alex will stop at nothing to keep Penny safe in his arms . . . as his claimed bride.

Editor's Note: Bring out the #PornCoc. Your week just got better!

I hope you'll enjoy the story as much I did writing it.

Warm regards,
Linzi Basset

Claimed Bride

Linzi Basset

CHAPTER ONE

"Drew Carver was killed in a motor vehicle accident last night."

Alexander Sinclair didn't react visually apart from his narrowing eyes. His steely gaze remained glued to the cityscape horizon. He stood in front of large picture windows—his usual spot when strategizing—in his luxurious office in Columbus Circle, New York.

"How sure are you it was an accident?"

His deep voice carried to Blake Harper, his friend as well as one of the shareholders in the company. Alex was a property mogul. He was the chairman and majority stakeholder in the Allied Group, a global property development firm he had founded at the young age of twenty-five. The company was best known for developing Time Warner Center, where their HQ was situated, as well as for the new Manhattan Redevelopment Project. According to Forbes magazine, Alex had a net worth of $5.5 billion. Alex was a philanthropist and a sports team owner too. He had recently bought a large stake in the NY Giants and the MetLife Stadium in East Rutherford. His generous donations and support to various welfare organizations had made him a sought-after businessman.

"According to the reports, he lost control of his vehicle as he approached the curve onto the Tappan Zee Bridge on Route 287. He went through the rails and into the Hudson river."

"Don't tell me. They couldn't recover the body?" Alex said cynically.

"Nope. They found his body alright. He's confirmed dead, Alex. He drowned. It seems he was on his way back to New York."

"Very convenient, wouldn't you agree?"

"Yes. I also have my doubts whether it was an accident but the witnesses on the scene couldn't confirm either way. It apparently happened too fast."

Alex sat down behind his desk. The dark mahogany surface gleamed in the sunlight streaking through the window.

"Who is the beneficiary of his life insurance?"

It was one of the fringe benefits all Alex's employees enjoyed—a lucrative pension fund and life insurance, differing with specific job level of each person. Drew Carver had been a top-level project manager at the firm and his beneficiary would receive about five million dollars.

"His wife, Penelope Carver."

Alex's brows drew together. "The same woman he claimed was the mastermind behind his fraudulent scheme?"

Blake shrugged. "If he was to be believed, yes but according to rumors I've just overheard, they've been separated for over a year."

"Based on what we know, it was probably a front to give their scheme more authenticity." Alex shook his head. The expression on his face turned dark. "How did we not see him for the con artist that he was, Blake? Normally our instincts are on point. I completely misjudged Drew Carver."

"He was a pathological liar, Alex. He manipulated everyone by burying his true self-expression and replaced it with a highly developed compensatory false self-confidence. We should've caught him earlier. He often came across as grandiose, self-absorbed, and conceited. I only realized it once we uncovered the fraud. He *lived* his lies, believed every word he said as true. We all fell for it."

"He was reasonably successful with all the projects he handled, so we had no reason to doubt him. The clients preferred to deal with him above other Project Managers. We missed it, Blake, because those traits never came to light when he was dealing with business. It was only outside of the office."

"And greed was the final contributor to his fall from grace. He thought he would be far away by the time we found out about it, especially as his reports indicated the deposits by the investors hadn't been paid yet."

"Which we had no reason to doubt. It was a stroke of luck that I bumped into Logan Burroughs at the airport. If not for that, we wouldn't have known the contracts for the development had been signed prematurely and deposits paid."

"Yeah, Drew was fucking clever, I'll give him that." Blake shifted in the chair. "What are we going to do? Drew disappeared with fifty-million dollars, Alex. That's not small change."

"No, it's not but at the time we restructured and upgraded our system, it opened a risk of security breach. You do recall that we invested in Crime Insurance four years ago to provide effective risk transfer against internal fraud."

Blake dragged his hand through his long hair. "I know," he said. "Still, are we just going to let it go like that? Allow little Mrs. Penelope Carver to live in the lap of luxury on our money? Just because her scheming husband got killed?"

"No, we're not. The Internal Forensic Team is already busy with an investigation. One way or the other, we'll track that money."

"What do we tell the investors?"

"Nothing. They don't need to know. We go ahead with the project. This time, I want you to take charge. It's a huge project. One we can't afford to fuck up." Alex picked up the folder his assistant had placed on his desk earlier. He uncapped his Mont Blanc. The signature he penned on the contract conveyed the silent fury that was curling deep inside him. "You'll have to inform his clients of his death and re-allocate his projects."

"Even the Chi Fung Foundation?"

Alex looked up. "Fuck! I forgot about that. It's one of our key re-development projects. One, I have personally already invested a lot of time and money in."

"Drew was the only one they were prepared to work with."

"Yeah." Alex dragged out the word, his expression turned pensive. "Because he was a 'happily married man' with a baby on the way. Family is inherently important to Zhang Wei Chén. He wouldn't think twice before tearing up that contract if he doesn't like Drew's replacement."

"We are the only ones who can handle this deal. Neither one of us is married nor, heaven forbid, have little brats running around our feet."

"No, we're not." Alex replaced the cap on the pen and leaned back in the chair. "Ask Drew's PA to bring me all the data they have on the Chinese project. Leave Zhang Wei Chén to me to deal with. In the meantime, find out everything you can about Penelope Carver and keep me up to date on funeral arrangements. We need to show our respect to our dearly departed employee and offer condolences to his grieving widow."

"May his soul rest in peace."

The somber tone of the priest droned on in the background. Penny had stopped listening when he began singing Drew Carver's praises. Her ex-husband, who she hadn't seen in over six months—ever since she'd obtained a restraining order against him. Their two-year marriage had been over for eighteen months already. The same amount of time they had been separated. She'd filed for divorce the day she'd realized what a scam artist he was, but he had refused to sign the papers. Instead, he'd begun hounding her, calling her, begging her to forgive him and take him back. He had suddenly had an epiphany that he'd been wrong and all that mattered was their love for each other.

Yeah, right, only you never loved me, you asshole. You were in love with my gran's money.

When he realized that Penny wasn't going to budge, he'd finally signed the papers. She had been a free woman a short two-weeks when she'd received the news that he'd been killed in a motor vehicle accident.

Penny had been shocked, but at the time, couldn't dredge up any sorrow over his death.

She still couldn't, even now . . . standing beside his grave. Bitterness flooded her as she watched the coffin slowly sink into the ground. She'd invested her heart and soul into their relationship. For a year he'd wooed her, treated her like a princess and she'd believed that she had found her soulmate.

Like hell I did. I wasted three years of my life!

She had been so stupid, so much in love that she'd blindly believed all his honey coated lies, of love and devotion. When he'd proposed they get married in Gran's hospital room, she never questioned his intentions. Her thoughts drifted back two years.

"Do you know what your gran's biggest wish is, darling?" Drew asked. He kissed the palm of her hand. His eyes were warm and engaging.

Penny felt tears burn behind her eyes. Her grandmother was the only family she had left and was on her deathbed, finally having lost the battle against lung cancer.

"I know what my wish for her is," she said in a trembling voice. Penny couldn't envision life without her. The woman had given up so much to support and look after her grandchild after Penny's parents had died in a boating accident. Penny had been eight years old.

Drew pulled her into his arms. *"I know it's difficult, darling, but you have to be strong for her."* He tilted back her head with a finger under her chin. *"The only thing she desires right now is to see you wed."*

Penny frowned. *"She hasn't said anything to me."*

"No, because she doesn't want to push you. How about it, Penny? We are planning to get married at some point, so why not now? At least you'll get to see how happy it makes Gran Erin."

Penny chewed on her lip as she considered Drew's proposal. She wasn't ready for marriage. Yes, she loved him and wanted to be his wife, but not yet. It was too soon.

"Maybe. But, you know I want my company in the black before we get married. I don't want to work long hours at the cost of our marriage."

"Don't you know I'll understand and support you, Penny? Isn't that what marriage is all about?" Drew kissed her deeply and gazed lovingly into her eyes. "I adore you, my Penelope, and neither of us is getting any younger. Will you please marry me?"

"Mrs. Carver?"

The priest's subdued tone yanked her from her musings.

"Yes, Father?"

He gestured toward the grave. Penny hesitated. Honoring Drew Carver, even in death, was something she didn't want to do. He'd killed any love or respect she had for him when he'd demanded half her inheritance the moment Gran's estate had been finalized. He'd turned into a greedy, uncaring and selfish man overnight. He'd finally admitted why he'd pursued and married her, when she refused to part with her inheritance.

"Why do you think I married you before she died, Penelope? As your husband it's my right!"

"No, Drew, it's not. Gran made sure of that. There's a stipulation in her will that my spouse has no claim to my inheritance, married or divorced, unless I willingly give it to them."

19

Drew had been furious. She cringed at the memory of his rage exploding. He'd hit her, cursing and accusing her of lying to him.

"I fucking wasted my time. A year! My skin crawled every time I touched you." He snorted. "I hate petite women and you . . . without your grandmother's money, you're worthless to me."

Penny shook off the dreary thoughts and walked closer to the grave. She picked up a handful of dirt.

"May your soul fry in hell, Drew Carver," she said sotto voce as she flung the dirt onto the descending coffin.

Penny turned and strode toward her car, her head held high. She didn't know anyone at the funeral, apart from Drew's cousin, who she'd only met once. She had no desire for small talk with any of them. The urge to get as far away from Drew Carver, even in death, was overwhelming.

He'd killed her spirit. The words, that she was worthless as a woman, had stuck in her mind. She'd lost all self-confidence then and hardly ever gone out since. It took her almost a year to realize what she was doing before she managed to pull herself out of the muck of unworthiness he'd buried her under.

Now, finally, she was free. Now, she could live life to the fullest.

"Mrs. Carver, one moment, please."

Penny stumbled to a halt. "Yes . . . *oh.*" Her lips formed a delightful round O as she pivoted around to face the man with a deep baritone dripping with self-confidence and power.

And promptly lost her breath.

She looked at his sinful mouth and couldn't take her eyes off the full lips that turned up a fraction. The words were already floating at her before she realized he was speaking again. She visibly shook herself.

Good lord, Penelope, get a grip. One would swear you've never seen an attractive man before.

Attractive maybe, but this man was drop-dead gorgeous and his voice tingled her nether regions. Entirely inappropriate, considering they were in a cemetery.

Penny took his proffered hand unconsciously. His fingers locked around hers, completely engulfing them in his own. His eyes flickered with interest when her lips opened in a gasping breath.

"I'm Alexander Sinclair. Drew worked for my company. I'd like to offer my condolences for your loss." He gestured toward her stomach. "I suppose the shock caused you to have a miscarriage?"

"A what?" Penny silently wondered if he had lost his marbles. She stared at him, still feeling the touch of his skin against her hand, tingling in a crackling frenzy.

"Drew told us you were pregnant," Alex drawled. His tone was laced with subdued bitterness and incredulity as he made the only assumption he could—another lie. He stared at her with quiet intensity. He didn't move; hadn't moved since the moment her soft, melodious voice had tantalized his senses. He found it difficult to wrap his mind around the knowledge that this petite, gorgeous and sexy-as-fuck woman, was a fraud.

"I'm afraid you have been misinformed, Mr. Sinclair," Penny said coldly.

She'd recognized the realization that dawned after the initial disbelief in his eyes. He was livid. Penny grimaced as he incinerated her with his fiery blue gaze. She couldn't look away, enraptured by the shade of his eyes—blue—like the sky, right before the sun disappeared; a dark, rich indigo, with specks of wild colors flashing due to the anger he didn't bother to hide.

His vision cleared seconds before his eyes narrowed to slits. Penny had an uncomfortable feeling that his anger was directed at her, which only enhanced the fascination she had for the drool worthy specimen that he was.

He was tall, dark, and handsome in a magnetic way. He was probably close to six feet, which made her feel even smaller. His dark brown hair was cut short on the sides but were longer at the top, giving him a naturally tousled look. He stared at her, down a straight aristocratic nose that sat over a wide sensual mouth with a lush bottom lip. She licked her own lips as the thought, of what his mouth would feel like, crossed her mind. His tall frame was set off by wide shoulders that filled the dark suit beautifully, probably hand tailored for him. She shivered at the thought of his strong arms, wrapped around her, dragging her against his hard torso. The thought evoked a ripple of excitement inside her throbbing loins.

Damn, this man looks good enough to eat.

Penelope! Concentrate!

"Ahem," Alex cleared his throat. The gruff sound was soaked with irritation.

Penny jerked her eyes back to his face from where her gaze had inadvertently gravitated toward the slight bulge in his pants. Her cheeks bloomed; caught staring at his crown jewels.

He took a step closer, his deep voice, low and muted, "Were we misinformed, Mrs. Carver, or was your husband?"

She stiffened visibly. The flash of heat directed his way was as sharp as a dagger, cutting through his resolve. Her voice clipped icily.

23

"I don't know what you're implying, Mr. Sinclair, but let me set you straight. Firstly, you should direct your condolences to Drew's cousin. He might care. I don't. Secondly," she held up her hand when his mouth opened. "Drew Carver wasn't my husband. I left him when I found out . . ." Her lips thinned. She tossed her hair back. "It took me eighteen months, but the divorce was finalized two weeks ago. Thirdly, I wouldn't have Drew's child even if he paid me ten million dollars."

"How about fifty million, Mrs. Carver."

Penny's eyes flashed to the man now standing next to Alexander Sinclair. Equally tall and just as attractive, she'd been too enraptured to pay him any attention until now.

"What are you implying and who the hell are you?"

"Blake Harper, Alex's partner."

"You know what, I don't care who or what either of you are. I don't owe you any explanation. Drew wasn't my responsibility and I don't want any part in the trouble he got himself into. Now, if you'll excuse me, I—"

"Mrs. Carver—"

"Oh, for goodness sake! Not another one," Penny snapped and spun around. "What do *you* want?"

She was too annoyed to be intimidated by the mammoth man facing her.

"I'm Agent Mark Farrow, FBI. I need you to come with me."

"Why? I haven't done anything wrong." Penny suddenly felt the world spinning around her.

"Then you have nothing to worry about. Shall we?" He stood to the side and gestured toward the black SUV standing at the curb.

"No, we shall not. Not until you tell me why the Federal Bureau is taking me into custody." Penny refused to budge. She might be petite, but she knew how to stand her ground.

"I am the senior agent in charge of the Corporate Criminal Fraud division of the FBI. Misuse of corporate property for personal gain and resultant tax violations are seen in a very serious light, Mrs. Carver. We have reason to believe that you were involved—"

"You're kidding, right?"

"I can assure you, Mrs. Carver, corporate fraud has the potential to cause immeasurable damage to U.S. economy and investor confidence. Now, please, let's go," Mark's voice deepened with authority.

"I'll follow you in my own car, Agent Farrow," Penny asserted. She dug out her keys from her bag.

"I'm afraid I must insist that you drive with me."

"Insist all you want. Unless you have a warrant to arrest me, I will follow you. I have done nothing wrong and being accused of criminal charges hasn't improved my day, Agent Farrow. Now, let's go. You're wasting my time."

Penny ignored the two men who were watching the interlude silently. From what Blake Harper had said, she had no doubt they knew exactly what was going on.

Which was a hell of a lot more than she did.

CHAPTER TWO

Padded black panels covered the walls. Penny assumed it had something to do with the acoustics of the room. She'd once read an article about the design of the FBI's interrogation rooms. A small rectangular window high up didn't offer any additional light to the room which was dimly lit. The chairs were comfortable but the steel table felt cold and forbidding under her hands. She sat facing a large tinted mirror wall which, she was relatively sure, offered the agent a front-row seat to her squirming.

Her gaze strayed to the clock above the door. Agent Farrow had kept her waiting for forty minutes already. She'd read more than enough thrillers to know that it was an interrogation technique to unsettle her.

"Of course, it only works on criminals, asshole," she mumbled. It had the opposite effect on Penny. She was becoming irritated and angry. She had a deadline which was looming around the corner.

Penny was living her childhood dream. One, she'd had since she was ten years old, ever since she'd started working with Gran, who used to make clothes for children. Penny, as it turned out, had a natural knack for design and Gran had been elated when she'd decided to study design at the school.

She loved the challenge of working with children clothes. Bit by bit, she's built her brand. Her designs were quirky and extremely sought after all over the globe. The inheritance that she'd received from Gran had offered her the opportunity to launch a children's clothing company, GenZ Designs. The kitschy, roller-skating unicorn logo had become her trademark. Her company designed and manufactured the clothes—in the US and Southeast Asia as well. The business was fast paced, with a lot of moving parts that required keen understanding. The Fall 2018 collection was due to release in three months and she was behind schedule.

She had considered not attending the funeral but an involuntary sense of loyalty had prompted her to go. Now, her entire day was ruined, and the clock just kept ticking.

"This is bullshit," she said. She pushed back the chair, intending to leave, when the door opened.

"My apologies for keeping you waiting, Mrs. Carver," Agent Farrow said. He sat down opposite her.

"Apology not accepted, Agent Farrow. You forced me to come here and then you deliberately keep me waiting, wasting my time. I resent being treated like a common criminal."

He didn't respond. His gaze lowered to the file he had placed on the table. He paged through the sheets of paper.

Penny bristled but determinedly kept her lips pressed shut. She'd made her irritation known. If he expected her to throw a tantrum, he was in for a surprise.

"Mrs. Carver, where is the money?"

Penny had already figured out that Drew must have been up to no good. What, she had no idea, or why *she* was being targeted as part of his underhanded scheme.

"I assume you're going to elaborate what money you are referring to?" Penny calmly folded her arms on her lap.

"Come now, Mrs. Carver. We both know you were co-conspiring with your husband in the fraudulent scheme. I'm referring to the fifty million dollars both of you stole from the Allied Group."

Penny flinched. She remembered the cynical accusation by Blake Harper at the cemetery for the same amount. She squared her shoulders.

"Tell me, Agent Farrow, how deep have you investigated my background?"

"I'm the one asking the questions, Mrs. Carver."

"Clearly, your team didn't do their homework properly. Drew and I are divorced."

"Very convenient, wouldn't you say?" His mouth twisted; the disbelief clearly discernible in his voice.

"For whom, Agent Farrow? Please, I'd love to know how you concluded that I am involved in Drew's scam. I don't need to steal from anyone. I have my own money. Lots of it."

"Greed knows no boundaries, Mrs. Carver." He brushed off her passionate defense. He tapped on the document in front of him. "If you and Drew were divorced, why did he call you daily for the past six months? Perhaps to discuss strategies?"

Penny blinked. "Really? How stupid do you think I am, Agent? Who in their right mind would discuss stealing a huge amount of money over phone? It sounds like you're grasping at straws *and* you're wasting my time." Penny got up. She flung her handbag over her shoulder.

"Sit down, Mrs. Carver or I will restrain you if necessary." He waited until she did as instructed. "Now, please answer my question."

"He was trying to convince me to withdraw the divorce application. Look . . ." Penny reached inside her bag. She slapped the restraining order in front of Mark. "I had to get a court order against him because he was becoming violent. I haven't seen Drew for over six months, nor do I have any idea what he had done with his life since I left him eighteen months ago."

A deep line formed between Mark's brows. He leaned on his elbows on the table.

"Your story doesn't corroborate with Drew's version, Mrs. Carver." His gaze bored into hers, searching her expression penetratingly.

"His version? You interrogated him before his death?"

"We had discussion with his employers and co-workers."

"And that would be the Allied Group?" Penny shook her head. "To be honest, Agent Farrow, last I knew, Drew was working for Goldstar Investors. I wasn't even aware that he had changed jobs."

The door opened after a brief knock echoed through the room. A blonde woman, dressed in a dark suit, entered briskly. She handed Mark a folder and left as quietly as she'd arrived. He glanced at the contents. Penny watched his lips flatten into a grim line. He looked at her; his eyes turned cold.

"If that is true, Mrs. Carver, how do you explain the two bank accounts recently opened in your name? One in the Caymans and one in Switzerland? With a total amount of forty-five-million dollars deposited six weeks ago."

Penny's jaw dropped.

"What?"

"You heard me." His cold gaze remained fixed on her.

Fury bubbled inside Penny. It was like a button had been pressed inside her brain; the primitive part that triggered fight-flight stimulus. Penny was a fighter. It hadn't been enough that Drew had almost destroyed her self-confidence; he had to drag her through this muck from his grave.

"If the bastard wasn't already dead, I would fucking kill him with my bare hands," she sneered. She clamped her fingers in a fist to stem the tremor that surged through her.

"How did you do it? It seems your husband, or rather, ex-husband, was closer to the truth than you care to admit. You were the one who masterminded the entire scheme."

Penny cast a skeptical look at Mark. "Is that what he said? I don't believe this. Look, Agent

Farrow, I left Drew because I realized he was nothing but a selfish scam artist, a low-life crook. I own my own business, a very successful and lucrative one at that. Why in god's name would I jeopardize that to help the man I despise more than anything?"

"I'd like to believe you, Mrs. Carver, but . . ." He tapped his index finger on the file. "Evidence tells a different story."

"I've never been to Switzerland or the Caymans. How could I have opened—"

"Both the accounts were opened online," he interrupted her gruffly.

"You're welcome to look through my laptop and every computer at my office, Agent Farrow. I am telling you, I had nothing to do with this. Questioning me for hours isn't going to change that."

"Excuse me, Agent Farrow," the blonde woman from earlier materialized once again. "A moment please."

He got up and followed her. "I'll be right back, Mrs. Carver."

Penny's shoulders slumped. She had never felt so lost and alone as she did at that moment. Even knowing how corrupt Drew was, didn't prepare her for the feeling of betrayal that swirled inside her.

"Six weeks? The money was deposited six weeks ago," she muttered to herself, suddenly realizing that it coincided with the signing of the divorce papers. He hadn't needed her anymore to get his hands on easy money. He had found a different avenue.

But he implicated me. Why? How could he be so unscrupulous to set me up to take the fall?

"I believe her."

Alex stared at Penny through the double-sided mirror. A sensation, similar to what he'd experienced when she'd turned to face him the first time, flowed through his body. It was a foreign feeling to Alex. He was the master of self-control and never submitted to any emotion, least of all, for the opposite sex. Oh, he loved women, lots of them, but it was a means to an end—sex, plain and simple, with no strings. He didn't know this woman from a bar of soap, but he couldn't deny the feelings he'd been experiencing since the first glance.

Get a grip Sinclair. It's nothing more than your dick talking.

She was drop-dead gorgeous and based on the conversation she'd just had with Mark—intelligent and whip-smart. His eyes narrowed when she glanced toward the mirror. Her soft, forest green eyes glinted in the overhead light. He recalled how the brown flecks circled her irises and then darkened when she got angry.

She tossed back her hair. He dragged in a breath at the sudden desire to get tangled in the luxurious strands of her shiny dark hair, the shade of melted chocolate, which framed her heart-shaped face. Her delicate jaw jutted out as she glanced at her watch—a sure sign of impatience. Her chest moved as she took a deep breath. His gaze inadvertently dropped to her full breasts that rose and fell softly as she exhaled. An errant pulse careened into his loins and jerked him out of the exquisite reverie.

He was shaken, realizing how badly he wanted this woman. More than he'd ever desired another.

And that's all it was. Lust. He contemplated the direction his thoughts were headed. Maybe that would be an effective way of getting information from her. *Hmm, yes, a very pleasant interrogation technique, for sure.*

"Strangely, I do too," Mark drawled. He joined Alex and Blake in front of the mirror. "Carver cleverly implicated her. It's either that, or she's an extremely gifted actress."

"If she's telling the truth, it means that Carver had an accomplice," Blake pondered aloud. "From what you told me about the deposits made into those two accounts, there's five million dollars missing."

"Yes, the thought crossed my mind as well. So far, we haven't been able to find any other money trail in his name." Mark frowned. "Agent Lilian managed to talk with the bankers in the Caymans and Switzerland. It seems Carver has safeguarded the money with a failsafe code that needs to be presented before any transaction can be made." He glanced at Alex. "And this is where I can't help but question her innocence. Both banks stated Penelope Rose Carver as the only beneficiary and the person most likely to know the code."

"That does changes this," Alex mused.

"I'm not sure," Blake interjected. "Remember what we discussed the other day, Alex. That man was clever, and in my opinion, maybe even a little psychotic. What if he used her as a front—setting her up to take the fall for him?"

"It's possible. It would've been easy enough for him to move the money as soon as he was in the clear," Mark agreed. "It also means that if she is innocent, she's in danger. As soon as the accomplice finds out Carver is dead, and that she might have the code, he would go after her."

"Then we need to get to it before he does," Blake said.

"She's becoming edgy," Alex observed, watching her shift in the chair and glance at her watch for the umpteenth time.

"I can't detain her much longer and I have no concrete reason to place her under arrest," Mark said.

"She needs to be told the entire story, Mark. It's important that she realizes there is real danger looming." Alex started toward the door. "Let me talk to her."

"You didn't exactly endear yourself to her at the cemetery, mate," Blake drawled.

Alex glanced at him from the doorway. "It won't be the first time I use my charm on a woman."

Mark and Blake laughed. "No, I guess not but somehow I don't think this little spitfire is going to be an easy conquest."

"Let me worry about that," he said as he walked down the hallway. Alex silently pushed open the door and stepped into the interrogation room.

"Look, Agent . . ." Penny swallowed the rest of the sentence when her eyes locked with his. He didn't miss the flare in her eyes or the way her breath faltered.

It was all the confirmation he needed to know that she wasn't immune to the attraction between them. Alex sat down. His expression remained impassive.

"You're wasting your time, Mr. Sinclair. I've answered Agent Farrow's questions. I have nothing further to say."

Penny resolutely folded her arms over her chest. She pressed her breasts flat, desperate to find a way to bring her wayward libido under control. She was shaken that her nipples had tightened into hard nubs as soon as he'd walked through the door. It was unsettling as much as it was exciting—the kind of feeling that she'd never experienced with Drew or any other man for that matter.

"No need to be defensive, Mrs. Carver. We want to believe you." Alex's deep, soothing voice invited her to trust in him.

"I find that hard to believe, Mr. Sinclair. Agent—"

"Alex."

"What?" Penny hated being interrupted.

"My name is Alex." His lips curved upward in an engaging grin.

Penny blinked at the transformation in his chiseled features, into a truly gorgeous specimen of a man, wondering how the hell she was supposed to concentrate when all she wanted to do was to lick his enticing bottom lip. Her tongue forayed over her plump lips, leaving them glistening. She bit back a groan as his eyes locked on her lips. It was more than a glance, it felt like a touch of his mouth against hers. It was echoed in the seductive promise in his gaze when he lifted his eyes.

"Mr. Sinclair, what exactly is it that you want from me?" Penny said bitingly—a defense mechanism to keep her wits.

She struggled to suppress the bloom of heat that began to sizzle deep inside her loins and festooned in a blush across her face. She portrayed, at best, a half-hearted attempt at being unaffected, when in fact she was overcome with lust.

"Was that a deliberate double entendre, Mrs. Carver?"

Penny's mouth gaped open, but before she could respond, he leaned closer. The tip of his finger gently pushed up her chin.

"As tempting as your plump lips are, you don't want an audience when I kiss you, sweetheart."

His fingers scorched her soft skin. Penny was shaken by the electric current that flowed through her body. It felt so good that it took every ounce of willpower to pull away from him.

"I'm not your sweetheart, Mr. Sinclair, nor will I ever be. And I have no desire to be kissed by you."

Penny silently cursed the croak that escaped from her lips. So much for trying to put him in his place!

The knowing grin on his lips attested to him calling her bluff. "Challenge accepted, sugar."

"I didn't . . . you . . ."

"Cat caught your tongue? Now, that would be a pity," he drawled in a velvety voice. His long arm reached across the table to draw his finger over her bottom lip. He pulled the pulpy flesh down. "Ah, there it is." His gaze blazed with blatant desire as he caught her eyes. His voice lowered to a whisper. "And I have every intention of tasting it, Mrs. Carver." His gaze slowly trailed over her face until it came to rest on her breasts. "As well as the rest of your charms."

The promise settled in a heavy throb in her lower body, leaving her trembling. The vision of the promise played like a movie trailer through her mind. She was more shaken than she cared to admit. Especially by the knowledge that had he leaned closer and kissed her, she would've reciprocated, irrespective of the audience on the other side of the mirror.

Alex leaned back in the chair. He stretched out his long legs, deliberately rubbing against her calves in the process. Her breath hissed from her throat. His smile broadened at the chilled look she aimed at him.

"Enough of trying to seduce me, Mrs. Carver. I need you to understand the danger you are in."

He ignored her indignant gasp. His voice was somber as he explained Drew's duplicity in detail.

"Are you suspecting that his death wasn't an accident?"

"The authorities have ruled it out but we're not so sure. Not after everything we've uncovered." Alex's gaze sharpened. "He set you up as a red herring to draw away attention from himself, but that also makes you a target for his accomplice."

"I don't understand."

Alex explained the situation with the banks. He pinned her with a direct stare. "Do you have any idea what code might be?"

Penny frowned. Her brain flailed to connect the dots of what she'd just heard. Her emotions were all over the place. She was hurt that Drew's betrayal went deep enough to put her life in danger while at the same time, she was furious that he had the audacity to use her. If she needed any further confirmation that Drew had never loved her, it was this. He'd had only one thing on his mind from the day they had met—money.

Penny drew a tired hand over her forehead. She had developed a throbbing headache.

"I don't know. It could be a number of things. I'll have to give it some thought." Her voice sounded trembling in her own ears. She avoided Alex's gaze as she rose. "I have to go."

"Penelope, haven't you heard anything I've just said? Your life could be in danger."

"Drew Carver has ruined three years of my life already. I am *not* going to allow him to take up one more second of my thoughts. If what you believe is true, I'm sure Agent Farrow can arrange for my protection. I'm leaving. I've had enough. I need to get out of here."

Penny tore out of the room, walking faster, until she was running down the hallway and out of the FBI building in Manhattan.

Chapter Three

"I need brunoised onion, celery and carrots."

Penny's pace didn't change. The knife hit the cutting board in rapid succession, slicing the onions lengthwise before she chopped them in equal sized cubes.

Amber Summers continued preparing the Thai coconut marinade for the chicken dish on the menu that evening. She was used to Penny dropping in at her restaurant, Amber's Cuisine, and helping in the kitchen. It was her stress reliever.

"At the rate you're going, we'll have enough mise en place for the rest of the month," Amber said drily. She eyed the growing mountain of vegetables in front of Penny on the counter.

"It's a poor fucking substitute, lemme tell you," Penny grumbled as she moved on to Shitake mushrooms. The knife flashed.

Once she escaped from the disturbing presence of Alexander Sinclair, she'd gone straight to the one place where she could find peace and strived to work through her thoughts.

"Wanna have a go at these?" Amber waved an oversized carrot in front of her nose. "Hm, a knobbed one at that. Perfect shape and size I'd say, to serve as a *substitute*."

Amber was concerned. She had wanted to accompany Penny to Drew's funeral, but she'd told her not to. To Penny, it was no more than an obligation. She had no intention of staying for the wake, but Amber hadn't expected her to arrive hours later in a state of silent rage.

They'd been friends for as long as she could remember. Their parents had been neighbors and the girls had been born two weeks apart. They had grown up together and were more like sisters than friends. No one else knew the other better than they did. They'd been through all kinds of heartache, joy and insecurities together. Amber would never forget how devastated Penny had been when she'd realized what a bastard her husband had actually been. Between the two of them, Penny had always been very careful with her heart. She didn't open up to love and emotions very easily. Drew had managed to get past the walls she'd built around her heart since her parents had died. His betrayal had turned the love she had for him to hate.

"No, I'll leave the carrots for *him*." Her voice lowered to a growl.

Amber noticed the rosy tint that bloomed over Penny's cheeks with interest. From her tone, Amber assumed the *him* wasn't Drew. She didn't say anything, knowing Penny would share her thoughts in her own time. She began to whisk together coconut milk, garlic, lime grass, chilies, galangal, brown sugar, salt, ginger, turmeric, cumin, coriander and cilantro.

"The fucking bastard set me up," she finally burst out. The knife hit the cutting board so hard, Amber expected it to split in two. "You know, I thought he couldn't sink any further in my eyes, but he proved me wrong, the rat bastard!" She waved the knife in the air. "If he wasn't already in his grave, I wouldn't hesitate to stomp him underfoot like the low-life deadbeat he was!"

Penny grabbed the carrot that Amber was waving in front of her nose once again. She slammed it on the chopping board. The knife came down and whacked it in two. One piece went flying like a cannonball and hit one of the sous chefs in the face. His surprised yelp echoed through the kitchen. Penny hardly noticed.

"And then he . . . *ugh*! I don't even have the words. He . . ." Another hard whack, another missile launched. This time the sous chef ducked. "He's just so . . . *so fucking* gorgeous." She put down the knife and looked at Amber. "There's attractive and then there's *attractive*. He just *whooshed* past that and blew my fucking mind!"

"I take it we're talking about two different people?" Amber's tone was dry.

"It's not fair to the female population that one man should be *so* hot and sexy," Penny continued unperturbed. "It's a crying shame to waste all that *good stuff* on one man, especially when he ends up being an arrogant pig." Her eyes widened when she noticed the heaps of vegetables on the counter, but she was on a roll. "And after *all that*, I still can't get rid of the tingling in my . . ." Penny looked around; her voice lowered to a whisper, "you know . . . my lady bits!"

Amber choked with laughter that threatened to escape. She stared at Penny, whose cheeks were blooming like tomatoes.

"I'm fucking *leaking*, Amber! My panties are soaked and every time I think of the demon, it just makes . . . dammit, Amber! It's *not* funny!"

Amber swallowed her laughter with much difficulty. "Are you gonna tell me who this demon of lust is?"

"Drew's boss, Alexander Sinclair."

Amber gaped at her. "*The* Alexander Sinclair? The one who just bought the New York Giants *and* the MetLife Stadium in East Rutherford? *That* Alex Sinclair?"

"I wouldn't know." Penny shrugged negligently.

"Good lord, woman! Under what rock have you been hiding all these years?"

"You know him?" Penny was rattled by the surge of jealousy that caroused through her.

"I know *of* him. I can't believe you don't. Sinclair is a big shot property developer and well-known for donating to various charities, among other things." Amber frowned. "Hang on. How did Drew end up working for him?"

"I have no idea. I didn't even know he had changed jobs." Penny slumped against the counter. "It's such a fuck-up."

"What? That you've got the hots for the boss of your deceased ex?"

"Ugh," Penny groaned. "Maybe if I got laid, he wouldn't affect me as much."

"C'mon, girl. What happened? Out with it." Amber looked around. The staff seemed very interested in their animated conversation. She hooked her arm into Penny's and dragged her toward her office. Once inside, she pushed her into a chair.

"Now, tell me. I'm sure we can work things out."

Penny exhaled slowly and then began to talk. She briefly summarized what had happened after the funeral.

"That fucking useless bastard! I've got a mind to dig him up and throttle him with my bare hands," Amber fumed. "I can't believe there was a time I actually liked the asshole!"

"They believe that Drew's accomplice might pose danger for me." Penny's tremulous voice was laden with fear and tiredness.

"Ya think! Forty-five-million isn't small change." Amber leaned forward. Her concern for Penny was shallow in her gaze. "Now what?"

"I don't know. I've been wracking my mind, but I can't begin to imagine what code Drew would've used. For that matter, why would he give me the power over it? Yes, I know, you don't have to say it. It was a scam but that doesn't make it any less confusing or infuriating."

Amber swiveled around in her chair. "This calls for some Dutch courage." She poured two glasses of single malt Macallan whisky and handed one tumbler to Penny. "Bottoms up."

They sipped the fiery liquid in silence; each entangled in their own thoughts.

"You're coming to stay with me until the FBI has sorted out this mess," Amber said with a decisive nod of her head.

"I refuse to allow Drew to rule my life from his grave, Amber. I won't be chased from my own home."

"Don't be foolish, Penny. You're in danger. You can't go home, and you know it. Besides, I won't allow it."

"Amber, you—"

A sharp rap on the door interrupted Penny as the sous chef peeked around the door.

"Yes, Craig?"

"Sorry to interrupt, boss." He smiled briefly at Amber. "Your dinner date has arrived, Mrs. Carver."

"My wh-at?" Penny choked on the amber liquid she'd just sipped.

"Mr. Sinclair. He's waiting for you at table six."

"Thanks, Craig," Amber excused him when she noticed Penny's gaping mouth. She leaned forward. "Holding out on me, girlfriend?"

"Me? No! I didn't tell him where I was going." Penny smoothed her hair with a trembling hand. "What the devil is he doing here? What am I saying? How in the hell did he know where to find me?"

Amber got up and strolled toward the door. She winked at Penny. "Well, come on then. I'm dying to see this gorgeous specimen who managed to defrost your ovaries."

"Very funny," Penny grumbled but dutifully followed Amber through the kitchen. She stood next to her, peeping through the swinging kitchen doors, into the restaurant.

"Holy crap. You were right. He's one hunk of a man. Quite drool worthy, I must say," Amber exclaimed. "One in a million-dollar-problem," she announced, tongue-in-cheek.

Penny couldn't drag her eyes from the man in question. She licked her lips, quite disturbed that Alexander Sinclair had the ability to make her forget her own name—by just sitting there; like the entire world was at his feet. She'd felt his compelling presence when he'd first introduced himself at the cemetery. He had an undeniable magnetism that she couldn't resist.

"I'm not going out there," she said decisively.

"Oh yes, you are." Amber promptly pushed her through the swivel doors. Penny stumbled forward. She spun around but Amber had already pulled closed the doors. She made big eyes at her and waved her off. "GO!"

Penny became aware that her abrupt entrance made her the object of the diners' curiosity.

She glowered at Amber and mouthed, "Traitor," which only drew a wide smile from her.

Penny inhaled, squared her shoulders and pivoted on her heel. Her steps were confident, but her thighs began to quiver when she became aware of the brooding look in Alex's eyes as he watched her approach. She tugged on the edge of the business-like black jacket that she'd paired up with a black pencil skirt for the funeral as she halted next to the table.

"What can I do for you, Mr. Sinclair?"

Alex leaned back against the padded leather booth. His eyes dropped to her mouth. Her stomach clenched in reaction. Not to mention the flush of heat soaking her panties—again! The move was deliberate. It effectively reminded her of his fingers on her lips.

"Alex, Penelope. Don't make me repeat myself again."

Her chin tilted in response. His eyes appreciated the dim overhead lights playing with her luxurious tresses as she tossed back her hair.

"You . . . I—"

"Cat catch your tongue again?" He didn't bother to hide his amusement. "Please sit down, Penelope. We need to talk."

Stubbornly, Penny didn't move. The high and mighty billionaire Sinclair had another thing coming if he thought he could order her around.

"Look, I've—"

"Sit down, Penelope, unless you want me to make a scene. Believe me, sweetheart, I would love to get my hands all over your delectable backside."

Her eyes narrowed in a silent battle of will. He moved his legs from under the table.

Penny scooted into the seat.

She might be defiant, but she wasn't stupid. The warning glint in Alex's eyes was promise enough.

Alex on the other hand, was silently delighted at Penny's blatant rebellion. It showed her strength of character and that she wouldn't be bulldozed into anything. That was a challenge. He was becoming more and more intrigued with her.

"Your wine, sir." William, one of the young waiters arrived at the table with the bottle that Alex had already ordered.

"It's your favorite, correct?" Alex asked as he gently swirled and sniffed at the offering before nodding at William.

Penny was stumped. Not only because he knew about her weakness for Prosecco but that he had taken the time to find out and not just gone ahead and ordered what he liked.

Men, in general, hadn't been considerate toward Penny. Not even Drew, during their happy times. She nodded when she noticed his lips quirk.

"You may pour, thank you, William."

"Do you wish to know the Chef's offerings for the evening, sir?" William asked as he filled their glasses.

Alex's gaze didn't waver from scrutinizing Penny.

"I don't believe that would be necessary. I believe Mrs. Carver will know what's the best."

William smiled at Penny. "Very well. Please let me know when you're ready to order." With a jaunty salute, he walked away.

Penny watched him go. Her eyes turned to Alex.

"How did you know where to find me?"

Alex took a sip of his wine. He contemplated her as he considered his answer. Penelope Carver wasn't the kind of woman who could be swayed with flattery. Considering the way her asshat husband had treated her, Alex knew instinctively that she would value honesty above everything else.

"There's not much I don't know about you, Penelope," he finally drawled.

"Because you believe I have your money?"

"No, sweetheart. Because you intrigue me."

"And I suppose I should feel flattered?" Penny was slightly annoyed that he didn't *show* any reciprocal attraction to her.

"That too, of course." His voice lowered suggestively but his expression remained enigmatic.

Penny opened her mouth but snapped it shut, knowing his comment had nothing to do with the question, rather with the wayward thoughts that kept popping up in her mind.

Get a grip, Penny! You're acting like a teenager crushing on a celebrity. Act your age, woman!

His ability to read her mind so easily was unsettling. She did her best to keep her expression impassive.

"So, you had me investigated?"

"Thoroughly."

"Why? You had no reason to suspect me. Not if you'd investigated Drew's background properly. He was always crooked." Penny couldn't hide the bitterness from her voice.

"He fooled all of us, Penelope. You're not alone."

Alex studied her thoughtfully while he took another sip of his chilled wine.

"You have excellent taste. This is a lovely wine." He straightened. "Drew's actions have left us wary, Penelope. I couldn't leave any stone unturned.

He didn't only steal from me; he betrayed his co-workers and our investors."

"How? I don't understand."

"Trust. It's very important in our trade."

"You can recover their trust. As soon as the money is returned to you."

"I'm afraid it's not that simple. We have an impeccable reputation and Drew's fraud can compromise that. We might still lose the project because of Drew's fraud."

"I'm not going to apologize on Drew's behalf, Mr. Sinclair. He was the embezzler. Not me."

"I don't expect you to."

"But you don't trust me."

"I didn't say that."

Penny took a long sip of her wine. She watched him over the rim of the glass.

"Then what are you saying? This is a FBI case, so why are you here?"

Alex picked up the menu. "I'm starving. Shall we order?"

"Look, Mr. Sinclair—"

"I told you to call me, Alex, Penelope."

"Why? It's not as though we'll ever be anything but acquaintances—at best."

He caught her hand in a tight grip. Watching her intently, he traced the creases on the inside of her palm. Her breath got caught in the back of her throat and her eyes widened. His provocative gesture was answered by a shimmering glint in her eyes. She squirmed in her seat, her hand steaming inside his. Alex felt his forehead tighten and his ears flatten against his head in response. A libidinous smile tiptoed across his mouth in expectation of a sizzling encounter with the worthy opponent Penelope was turning out to be. He felt his groin tighten as he watched her pink tongue brush her lips with a sensuous flick.

Penny's stomach lurched as she identified the predatory gleam in his eyes.

"We don't know each other well—yet—but I expect you to be honest with yourself, at least, if not to me, Penelope. You know, as well as I do, that we're on the precipice of an explosive relationship."

"We are?"

The smooth husky tone of her voice tore a rich seam of lust in him. It wrapped tightly around Alex's loins, sending ripples of heat spiking through his body. He found it incomprehensible that his testosterone reacted so strongly to her. It was a feeling he'd come to believe he'd never experience. Oh yes, beautiful women turned him on, but this? It was on a level that made him feel like he was riding a wave of adrenaline.

"Yes, we are. We'll talk, honey, but first you have to feed me."

Penny didn't need a mirror to know that her cheeks were blooming at the double entendre. Visions of her *feeding* him flashed through her mind. She pressed her thighs together in a desperate attempt to keep her sexual excitement contained. Never had she felt such an instantaneous chemical attraction and reckless impulsiveness to be intimately possessed by a man. It was scary but exciting as hell.

Alex's chuckle sounded wicked and promising at the same time. "You have a one-track mind, Penelope. Not that I mind, of course, but I can't help but wonder. Is it because you've not had sex for a while or because you are hot for me?"

"Don't flatter yourself," Penny mumbled. She yanked her hand from his to grab the menu, trying to hide her heated countenance. "Pierogies with sour cream and caramelized onions are my favorite appetizer. For the entree the 'Pollo al forno', Amber's signature chicken dish, is served with a salsa verde full of anchovies and capers. It's to die for."

Alex allowed Penny a reprieve. He signaled William over and placed their order. Sipping on his wine, Alex leaned back.

"Tell me about yourself."

"What's there to tell that you haven't already found out yourself?"

"Come now, sweetie. The information I have on you is background. I want to know about you. Your likes, dislikes, your goals and dreams."

Penny stared at him trying to solve the puzzle that was Alexander Sinclair and how he affected her life.

"Very well, but only if you reciprocate."

"Of course. Tell me about growing up."

Penny laughed. "You're not serious."

"I'm not?" He said enigmatically. "I want to know all there is about your life, Penelope. Like I said, we're going to be spending time together."

"Of course, we are," Penny didn't bother to hide her cynicism. Little old Penelope Carver and the billionaire businessman, Alexander Sinclair? Not a chance in hell, that was for sure. They were like chalk and cheese.

Penny started talking. She was amazed at how easy it was to share her life story with him. Maybe it was because he seemed genuinely interested. The dinner turned into a very pleasant evening.

Until she stood up to leave.

"I'm afraid I can't let you go, Penelope."

"And why not?"

"Because you're not safe. For as long as Drew's co-conspirator is out there, you will be under my protection."

"That's absurd. Besides, Amber has already offered that I stay with her."

"And you don't think, whoever it is, won't look for you there first? Do you want to put your friend's life in jeopardy as well?"

Penny hesitated. She had honestly not considered that but staying under Alex's roof was out of the question.

Totally and completely not an option!

"What about a safe house? Doesn't the FBI place people like me under protective custody?"

"I'm it, Penelope. I volunteered my services." He took her arm and nudged her toward the kitchen. "I imagine you'd like to say goodbye to Amber." He smiled at her. "And I'd like to meet her."

CHAPTER FOUR

"And?" Blake asked as he pushed past Alex, the moment he opened the front door to his home in Gibson Beach in Sagaponack, ranked as the richest suburb in New York.

"And what?"

Alex closed the door before he followed Blake into the den. He found him fixing two drinks.

"Did you manage to win her trust?"

"Was there any doubt that I would?"

Blake handed him the drink. "So, where is she?"

"Upstairs."

Blake's expression didn't change, although the flare in his eyes conveyed his surprise.

"You brought her home with you?"

Alex took a deep swig of the scotch, swirling the soothing taste around in his mouth. His gaze remained on the clear amber liquid in the glass. "She serves multiple purposes."

"Please, do enlighten me."

"We need her to recover the money and regain our clients' trust. Secondly, she's the key to keeping the Chi Fung Foundation invested in us as their partners in the Chinatown project."

"How exactly do you figure that?"

"Chinese culture values family above all else. It's the only reason they agreed with Drew and decided to sign with us for the project."

"Because they thought he was blissfully married with a baby on the way."

"Exactly. Because the project is about providing the Chinatown community a better life, the foundation wants to be assured that their family values are shared by their partners on this project."

"How exactly does Drew's ex-wife fit into this picture?"

"Zhang Wei Chén wants a happy family man. I'm going to give him what he wants."

"Oh, hell no!" Blake gaped at Alex.

"Oh hell, yes."

"You're not serious, Alex. You, of all people?"

"Yes mate, me. Mrs. Penelope Carver is about to become my wife."

Blake barked out a short, disbelieving laugh. "Lemme guess. She was delighted at the prospect."

"Not exactly." Alex swallowed the last of his drink. "She doesn't know about it—yet."

Blake searched Alex's expression speculatively. "Are you going to tell her or seduce her into wedded bliss?"

Alex shot him a disgruntled glance. "You know why I have never had any interest in getting married, Blake. For one thing, women expect love and devotion. Both traits don't exist outside of romance novels."

"So, how do you plan on winning her over? Especially after the callous way Drew had treated her."

"*Because* of how he'd treated her, it'll be easy to get her to agree to a temporary arrangement."

"Ah, so the marriage will be annulled as soon as the Chinatown project is finalized?"

"Yes. I have no intention of playing house forever."

"You're forgetting one thing, mate. Zhang is very astute. How are you gonna get around the fact that he wants a family man?"

"Give him what he wants."

"Hold on there, Alex! This puts an entire new dimension on your scheme. You intend to make her pregnant and then walk away from your own child? You might not believe in love, my friend, but leaving behind your own flesh and blood? Not even you'd be able to do that," Blake said in quiet tones.

"Nor do I have any intention to. It's the perfect solution, which will never come to fruition otherwise, Blake. I get the thing I'd love to have without the added aggravation of a nagging wife—a son."

"And what if it's a girl?"

Alex shrugged. "Then I'll love her just as much."

"How do you know she'd even agree to having your child? You heard what she'd told Mark during the interrogation. That she had no interest in giving Drew a child."

"Because she had realized he was only using her."

"You're not much different here, mate."

"No. She'll know exactly what's in store for her once she agrees to my proposal." Alex pushed aside the guilt that gnawed at him. Blake didn't need to know exactly how he planned to get Penelope to agree to marrying him.

So, there Penny was. Less than thirty minutes after saying goodbye to Amber, settled in Alexander Sinclair's house, or more accurately, his three-story mansion. Although it was filled with everything luxurious, it looked and felt homely. A house made for a family. To be filled with love, happiness and laughter.

Of course, Amber had played a crucial role in her being there.

"Traitor!" Penny muttered as she walked into the bathroom. Her lifelong friend had happily thrown her to the wolves by wholeheartedly agreeing with Alex.

"Holy shit!" She'd stared around in amazement.

The posh bathroom looked more like a spa and was probably larger than her own bedroom and bathroom combined in her upmarket penthouse in Manhattan. The walls were a delicious shade of apricot and the floor Calacatta marble. "Oh, my," she drooled over the massive oval bath in the center of the room, envisioning sinking into its depths. Beautifully framed mirrors reflected at her from all around the room. There was even a big plush ottoman in one corner. She couldn't resist lighting the candles on either side of the bath and the vanity table before she quickly filled the tub. The flickering flames shrouded the room in a seductive ambience as she sank into the foaming bubbles.

"Ah, heaven," she sighed blissfully.

It didn't take long for the heat and steam to lull her into complete relaxation. Her eyes fluttered closed. Her body slowly slipped lower. She came up sputtering as water filled her nostrils.

"Very clever, Penelope," she coughed. She briskly finished bathing. She hadn't realized just how tiring and stressful the day had been.

"Hopefully, I'll be able to sleep soundly tonight," she sighed as she drained the tub, dried up and climbed into the oversized bed. Insomnia had been her constant companion since she'd left Drew. She'd hoped that moving on will improve her sleeping habits. So far, it was still an elusive wish. She was still sifting through her thoughts for the code when she drifted into a deep slumber.

Penny was sleeping so soundly that she was blissfully unaware of the man who walked in barefoot, with a towel wrapped around his waist, into her room thirty minutes later.

The balcony door and curtains were open to allow the cooling breeze into the room. Alex stood staring at the sleeping woman, illuminated by the soft, silvery moonbeams, radiating a divine aura around her. The muted spotlight painted her in a hypnotic glow.

Alex hadn't planned on coming to her room but had unconsciously found himself there, next to the bed; slowly running his eyes over her beautiful face. Her hair fanned out across the pillow. He couldn't resist the allure and reached out to run his fingers through the silky strands. She looked so innocent, vulnerable even, with her hand tucked beneath her cheek, and long lashes dusting her rosy cheeks.

She moaned softly as she turned onto her back. The sheet fell to her waist, leaving bare a pair of gorgeous, rounded breasts to his blazing gaze. Her free hand moved to cup one breast; her fingers framing the rosy nipple. Alex had never seen anything more seductive than the vision he was presented with in that moment.

His hand lifted, as if of its own accord, to softly caress her cheek. He trailed his fingertips over the slope of her breast and gently circled a succulent nipple. Heat settled in his loins, his cock started a slow, heavy throb as he watched the twin nubs grow taut. He continued his quest, sliding his hand over her waist to fold around the curve of her hip. She sighed, turned and pulled the sheet up to hide the seductive treasures from his hungry eyes.

Alex dragged in a tortured breath, knowing a cold shower was imminent if he intended to get any sleep.

Penny yawned as she walked into the bathroom the next morning.

"Oh," she gasped. She stumbled to a halt as she caught Alex's scorching gaze in the mirror. His eyes remained glued on her even as he continued to wipe the leftover shaving cream from his face. Penny stood frozen to the spot, gobsmacked at the rippling muscles, laid bare to her gaze. Naked, his shoulders appeared even larger, his back wide and sculpted— a perfect T-shape as it narrowed into slim hips and scrumptious, rounded buttocks.

Such a pity the juicy parts are covered with a towel.

She felt a ripple of excitement course down her spine when Alex's eyes did a slow forage over her breasts which, she belatedly realized, were naked. She had gone to bed only in a pair of lace panties. She could feel a heated rosy flush blooming over her body. Still, she was glued to the spot as she watched him staring at her breasts. Her nipples turned painfully taut under his gaze.

Alex didn't turn but allowed his eyes to soak up her near-nakedness. The allure of her lush beauty weakened his knees. Her full breasts made his mouth water. His gaze slid lower over her toned stomach and white lace panties, which fitted snugly around her slim hips. The material did more to entice than hide. The inviting shadows between her thighs beckoned him. His cock twitched in eager anticipation.

He threw down the towel and turned around.

Penny retreated. She licked her lips and croaked, "I'm sorry. I didn't realize we had a connecting bathroom. I'll just leave."

She groped for the door handle but before she could find it, Alex was there, flattening his palms against the door on either side of her; effectively imprisoning her with his body.

"Going somewhere, honey?"

"I . . ." Penny blinked owlishly; unable to draw her gaze from his mouth that was coming closer with each passing second.

His eyes darkened as he looked her over.

"So beautiful." He traced the slope of her small nose to her pouty lips, which seemingly was too much for him. With a wicked grin, he fitted her against him. Their groans echoed in the room as hard muscles met soft curves.

Penny was enraptured by his lips moving closer, almost in slow motion. Her hands tightened into fists. Her stomach was tied in a knot of anticipation. This was what she'd been waiting for.

If she was honest, she'd been yearning to feel his skin against hers, his lips taking possession of hers.

Then his lips brushed over hers, feathery soft, teasing and so inviting, Penny had to force back the desire to lay claim to his lips. Her breath rushed through her slightly parted lips, mingling with his in that split second before he sealed the space between them and kissed her deeply.

Oh, sweet heaven. This man knows how to kiss.

Penny was flooded with sensations running rife through her body. How was it possible that he awakened emotions inside her so quickly? With a single kiss the world around her spun wildly. It was more than desire. It was a deeply rooted need coiling inside her mind, capturing her heart and her soul. She had denied those needs for the longest time. Now, it burst to the surface like coming back to life. She *needed* him. Somehow, her body and mind had already decided it wanted Alexander Sinclair.

Alex exulted in her capitulation to his demanding kiss as he felt her hands wrap around his waist. She pressed herself harder against his body. He guided her undulating hips in a seductive dance against his rising arousal. There was nothing in his mind at that moment, but her. He watched her and imagined burying his cock deep inside her tight heat. He was startled at the uninhibited passion that engulfed their kiss, followed by an unwanted stirring of emotion deep in his heart.

He had always reveled in the fact that he was untouchable, unreachable. He'd built himself that way. Growing up while watching his mother struggle to make ends meet after his father had walked away from them, had taught him early on that love and happily-ever-after didn't exist. That it was the root of heartache and regret. He'd built the impenetrable wall around his heart, brick by painful brick. Nothing and no one could break through.

Except in this moment, he felt a tiny crack begin to form. He wasn't sure how to react, it was a foreign feeling to him; one, he had no intention of indulging in. He deliberately closed his mind against the confluence of emotions.

His breath wheezed through his teeth as her fingers fluttered over his torso, his narrow waist, his corrugated abs and his muscled back.

"You're playing with fire, Penelope," he growled as he placed nibbling kisses on her chin. Her breath caught as he sucked on her bottom lip. He caught her hand in his when it ambled toward his throbbing, tumescent tool.

"Oh no, sweetie. You don't get to dictate where this is going."

"And what exactly is *this*?" Penny puffed in a breathless whisper.

"This, Penelope, is an introduction." His voice thrilled with an undertone of domination. Penny was caught by a tremor of excitement that toggled deep inside her loins. The heavy throb of her clitoris was electrifying as he slowly pushed her legs apart with his knees. His hands anchored her against the door as he watched her eyes flare when he pressed his hard cock against her pulsing core.

"Of what?"

Penny couldn't deny the excitement she felt, being at his mercy. It felt good to be desired after a long abstinence. She sighed as he kissed the tender skin between her breasts, slowly dragging his wicked tongue downward until he placed soft kisses on the rounded curve of her breast.

"Your taste, luv, on my tongue." His breath tickled the hardening tips of her breasts. He slowly traced the soft slope of her breasts with his fingertips while he left a trail of wet kisses from the one breast to the other; teasingly, closer to the tips that were already taut with desire.

"And I have to say, luv. You taste divine," he murmured, his hot breath enticing the aching nub with a promise of what was to come.

"Mr. Sincl-air . . ." Penny begged brokenly; swamped by the desire to have his mouth on her nipples.

Alex stiffened. He pulled back with his brow furrowed. His mouth turned grim. "What's my name, Penelope?"

"I . . ." Penny glanced at him. Her gaze flickered as she read the angry reproach in his eyes. "Alex," she finally allowed his name to fall from her lips. It felt right, like she'd known it would, which was why she'd refused to use it. Till now.

"Say it again."

"Alex, please." Her lashes swept up as she blinked pleadingly.

His voice lowered. It flowed over Penny with the smooth richness of aged whiskey. "Please what, luv?"

"You know . . ." she said haltingly. Penny had always been shy when it came to intimacy and had never taken the initiative. She'd never asked for anything either. Maybe because in her very limited experience, no man could arouse her as skillfully and as quickly as Alex had. Now, she felt the need throb through her body; a need to be devoured by him, to become a vessel for his desire.

"Ah yes, Penelope, I think I do. The question is, do *you* know what it is you're getting yourself into?"

"What do you mean?" Penny had a hard time shifting gears. Her nipples throbbed under his continued caresses on her breasts.

"This," Alex pointed between them. "You and me. Do you honestly think a quick fuck is going to satisfy me, little one?"

"I—"

He leaned closer, growling as she arched into his tongue when it teased her nipple with languid, laving motions, his palm brushing with feathery lightness over the other. He continued the barely-there touch, alternately touching and licking from the one nipple to the other.

"Because, let me make one thing abundantly clear, luv," he murmured against her breast. He tortured her a moment longer and then, with a salacious lick, finally pulled the nub deep into his mouth. He sucked on it with long, deep motions— pulling her entire globe upward. Penny purred, and then mewled like a kitten when he feasted like a starving man on its twin.

Alex pushed her legs further apart and slipped his fingers underneath her lace panties. He found the treasure between her legs; pleased that her labia were already soaked in honeyed juices.

"Oh lord," she whimpered when he nibbled on her nipples while spreading her nether lips apart.

She lifted one leg to lock it around his waist. He dipped a finger inside, wetting it, to spread the moistness around her clit.

"Holy shit!" Penny jerked against his hand when he immediately started to rub it with quick, hard motions. With his mouth attached to her burgeoning breasts and his fingers wreaking havoc to her body, Alex played her like a string guitar. It shouldn't surprise her. He was the master of the game; knew how to get her off quickly, which he achieved within moments. Before she could even comprehend, the heat flushed her chest, her body bowed, and a low scream echoed in the room.

"Ohgodohgod!" she cried, desperately trying to breathe as he bit hard into her nipple. The stinging pain set her clit tingling even more under his fingers which ruthlessly fed the waves of pleasure, tumbling her in rapture that rocked her entire body.

"Yes, Penelope. That's what I wanted you to know. Look at me," he growled as she continued to pant and claw at his shoulders.

Her eyes lifted to his, smoky and filled with the pleasure that was still wracking her body.

"Are you listening to me, Penelope?"

"Yes," she said in a breathless whisper. His penetrating gaze probed her with such intent, she couldn't look away.

"I don't just want a fuck buddy, Penelope. I can get one of those anywhere, anytime. I want more with you. Once you figure out what it is I want, then and only then, will I give your body what it truly craves."

"And what is that?"

"My cock, pounding you—hard, deep and without mercy—as I lay claim to your delectable body. Because until then, my sweet Penelope, I will only wet your appetite, not satiate it."

"You don't know what I need." Penny pushed him away as she desperately tried to gather the frayed edges of her mind. She couldn't recall if she'd ever come as hard as he'd just made her climax.

"Ah, but I believe I do, luv. You need to be sexually and emotionally satisfied. Something, your reaction just now proved, you'd never truly experienced."

"And I suppose you have the magic touch."

"I don't know about that, Penelope but what I do know is that your body is in tune with mine, as mine is with yours." He pressed his face closer to hers. His eyes glowed like gems. "And that tells me that I'm the only one who can give you the satisfaction you need."

Penny finally managed to gather her wits. She was mortified that she'd fallen at his feet like a lovestruck hussy. Her voice was cold in an attempt to save face.

"Don't bet on it, Mr. Sinclair. I haven't had sex for years, so at this point, anyone will be able to satisfy me."

She opened the door and flung a glare over her shoulders at him that traveled with unnerving thoroughness over his muscled frame.

"Needless to say, you are hot as fuck, Mr. Sinclair, but way too vain for my taste. So, thanks, but no thanks. I'll rather find another hot body to ease my lusts."

Penny pulled the door closed behind her as she stepped into the bedroom. She bristled as his deep chuckle echoed through the door, followed by what sounded like a vow.

"Challenge accepted, luv."

CHAPTER FIVE

"That fucking bastard!"

The cell phone clattered on the table. Her hands trembled, and she could feel her cheeks heat up with the malevolence that boiled inside her. Her usually beautiful face was pulled into a grimace that gave away the biliousness of her true nature.

"I can't believe I was stupid enough to believe every fucking word you said to me, you fucktard! I even blew the only chance to rein in the most eligible bachelor in New York City and for what—a fucking lousy five million dollars?"

The droll voice of the bank manager at the Cayman National Bank replayed in her mind.

"I'm sorry, Mrs. Carver but as you are aware, you and your husband made this stipulation yourselves when you opened the account. Unless you are personally present to verify your fingerprints and the failsafe code, my hands are tied. I'm afraid I can't release the funds."

"But my husband is dead. I'm too distraught to travel that far at the moment and I need the money to settle his estate," she protested in a wailing voice.

"I am terribly sorry for your loss, madam, but I can't bypass our clients' stipulations. Our bank is very strict about that."

A similar conversation had followed with CIM Bank in Switzerland. She was livid that Drew Carver had betrayed her trust. He had been an easy target. Since the first day she met him when he'd come to her office to sign his employment contract, she'd known it would be a piece of cake to manipulate him. All senior recruits at the Allied Group signed their contracts with the Group's attorney.

It hadn't taken much manipulating, for that matter. He had jumped at the opportunity with greedy enthusiasm. She should've recognized his true nature for what it was. A pathological liar. She should know. It took one to know one. She should've taken more caution while planning the embezzlement, but he had been a charmer on top of it and—

"Fuck! Fuck! What the am I going to do now? I have to find a way to get my hands on the rest of the money. Why Drew? Why involve your prissy little ex-wife?"

Gabrielle Brittle was a beautiful woman but cold as the Antarctic. Someone had once said that she had ice in her veins. She had always been driven to succeed and the day she'd signed on as Alexander Sinclair's attorney, it had been the highlight of her career. She'd carefully kept their relationship professional, while at the same time, she used her charm, trying to beguile him. He'd reacted exactly the way she'd wanted. He had been intrigued. He still was, but her desire for immediate riches had come in the way. If he found out that she had been the mastermind behind Drew's fraud, her career and any hopes of becoming Mrs. Alexander Sinclair were over. In the meantime, she had to find a way to get to the money to ensure anonymity.

"Think! There has to be a way to get that fucking code."

She sat down behind her desk and started a search on Penelope Carver.

"Nothing. Little Miss Goody-Two-Shoes doesn't even have a parking ticket," she snarled an hour later. "Nothing I can use." She slammed her fist on the desk. "But that's not going to stop me. I didn't put my reputation on the line for fucking nothing. One way or the other, I will get that money. It's mine! It was *my* plan. I'm the one who deserves it. With it in my pocket, I'll be in Alexander Sinclair's league and then nothing will stand in my way."

She began pacing again. Her heels clattered on the mahogany floor as she paced back and forth. One thing kept niggling at her. Why Penelope Carver? Drew had agreed to the divorce her the minute their plans had been airtight and he was guaranteed of his twenty percent share. It didn't make sense. The decision to deposit the money in his name had been strategic. Gabrielle wanted to make sure it was a clean swipe before she claimed her share. If not . . . well, then Drew would've taken the blame. Except, he ended up dead and now she stood the chance of losing everything anyway.

"Wait a minute! What if he was scamming me all along? What if she was in on it and he used the divorce to sideline me? Fuck!"

She scrolled through the contact list on her cell phone and tapped the one she was looking for. Her long fingernails did a rat-a-tat on the desk as she waited impatiently.

"Yes. I need you to do something," she said without preamble. "I want everything you can find on Drew's ex-wife. Everything, including who her friends are and what habits she has."

"What for?" A deep voice grated in her ear. "He's dead, what does she have to do with anything?"

"Just do what I say, Clive. Without her, we're screwed."

A sharp rap on the door drew her attention as it opened to allow entrance to her assistant.

"I need that information yesterday. Time is of the essence." Gabrielle ended the call. "Yes, Anne?"

"If you don't leave now, you'll be late for court."

Gabrielle glanced at her watch. "Shit. I didn't realize it was so late." She got up and pulled on the dark business suit jacket Anne held out to her. She took the proffered briefcase and headed for the door.

"Are the paralegals ready?"

"John and Sara are already there to set up the presentation boards like you requested. This case will put your name right up there with the big five," Anne said as she tugged on Gabrielle's jacket.

"I should hope so, but first, I need to win."

"Zhang was very upset with the news of Carver's demise," Blake reported as he walked into Alex's office.

"I told you to leave him to me."

"Gavin transferred the call to me. You were in a meeting with Holden's executives for the Manhattan Mall project."

Alex sighed heavily. "We should've contacted Zhang the moment we found out about Drew's fuckup. No matter what we do now, it's going to appear as an afterthought."

"He already indicated that he may schedule a meeting with Galaxy Development Group. So, unless you've got Drew's little ex-wife tied with the proverbial ball and chain, we're screwed, mate."

"You know that it's too soon, Blake. If I rush her, it'll blow up in my face. Besides, Zhang signed an agreement with us, which Gabrielle made sure was airtight. Drew's death isn't adequate reason for him to ditch us in favor of another developer."

Alex threw down his pen. His glance flickered over the busy street far below. "What was Zhang's reaction?"

"I didn't elaborate, only that he'd passed away in a motor vehicle accident. He was shocked. I got the impression that there was more to his call but I couldn't put my finger on it."

"Galaxy has been trying to get in on this project from day one. We both know they won't think twice before playing dirty. Did Zhang say how much longer he'll be in the US?"

"Two months max. He had called to arrange a meeting with Drew to discuss the designs with the architects. He wants to ensure that the project is well under way before he returns to China."

"Very well. Can you arrange a dinner with him and his wife—next week, Friday? You, me and my fiancée, Penelope Winters."

"Winters?"

"It's her maiden name. Based on the reports of her background check, she's in the process of reverting back to her maiden name. I don't want Zhang to know she's Drew's ex."

"Of course not. Imagine his reaction if Drew's picture-perfect familial bliss arrived on your arm, two weeks after his death."

"Exactly."

"You do know that Carver's name will come up during the course of the evening?"

"Don't worry, mate. I'll make sure my future wife is well prepared . . . and willing to play her part." He tapped his fingers on his desk. "It might be a good idea for you to bring along a date; one willing to play the role of your committed girlfriend."

"You're kidding, right? Me, a girlfriend? I haven't had one of those since college. Like you, I prefer playing the field too much."

"It'll be just one night, Blake. I'm sure you'll survive."

"Yeah, I guess I will."

Gavin Roux, Alex's assistant, popped his head around the door. "Mark Farrow is here, Alex. He asked if you have a moment to spare?"

"Of course, show him in."

Not only was Mark a senior FBI agent dealing with the fraud case, he was also a very good friend of Alex and Blake from college days and completed the trio. The tabloids like to call them the Rogues of Manhattan, seeing as they played the field together.

"You guys up for lunch? I have something to discuss with you but I'm starving too," Mark said by way of greeting as he strode through the door. With his six-foot-three frame and muscled built, he was always hungry.

"Why am I not surprised that food is the first thing on your mind when you walk in here?" Alex drawled.

"Because it's the *only* thing that's ever on his mind," Blake quipped.

"Not true. Most of the time I have sultry seductive blondes on my mind."

Alex shrugged on his jacket as they prepared to leave. "You know, now that I think about it, for a man who has a fixation for blondes, why is it that you always have a brunette or a redhead on your arm?"

Mark's broad shoulders rolled in a negligent shrug. "I'm looking for the right blonde. Until then, I'll play with their gorgeous counterparts."

"Yeah, mate, that's bloody convenient."

The banter continued until they were seated at one of the restaurant's they favored, around the corner from Alex's office in Manhattan.

"A woman contacted the offshore banks this morning, claiming to be Penelope Carver," Mark stated as soon as they placed their orders. "They've been placed on alert."

"A woman claiming to be her, or do you believe it was Penelope?" Blake asked in between taking a sip of his wine.

"There's no way to tell for sure. Although they have agreed to divulge certain information, both banks are relatively protective of their clients. Besides, none of them would know for sure." Mark glanced at Alex. "What do you think? You've spent some time with her; do you still believe she's innocent?"

Alex pondered the question. Penny's face flashed through his mind. Her sweet submission and almost *innocent* response earlier in the bathroom had been on his mind the entire day. He usually had a sixth sense about people. With

Penelope, he was concerned that his testosterone might be getting in the way of his thinking.

"You've got the hots for her, don't you? It's more than just protecting her that made you offer to keep her, isn't it?" Mark prodded.

"Maybe. But that doesn't mean I'm blind to the possibility that she might be a very apt liar." A frown pulled Alex's brows together. "Since we've uncovered his scam, I've come to look at him in a different light. He doesn't seem to be the type to trust a woman. He was too much of a chauvinist."

"Which means, you're wondering if it wasn't Penelope who made that call, after all," Blake interjected.

"It might very well be," Alex conceded. "Who knows, she may have wanted to verify what we've been saying and made the call to see if there was any truth in it."

"I'd agree if she only phoned one bank but this woman phoned both and tried her best to get them to release the funds without her meeting the failsafe requirements." Mark buttered a warm bread roll. He dragged in the fresh smell of fresh baked bread. "Hmm, heaven."

"Have they given you an indication what the failsafe entails?" Alex asked as he chewed thoughtfully on a piece of bread.

"A unique code needs to be supplied but here's the trick—Mrs. Carver must personally present herself at the banks for fingerprint verification."

Alex went cold. He didn't want to believe that Penelope might have been lying to him. "Which means she would've had to be there to register her fingerprints in the first place."

"Not necessarily. They accept a police-verified biometric data. It's a normal practice for off-shore banks," Mark said. "Besides, we checked the passenger list of all airlines flying into the Cayman's and Switzerland around the time the account was opened. She definitely wasn't on one of them. As a matter of fact, the full background check on her movements confirmed it."

"Am I the only one who is wondering if his co-conspirator is a woman, exactly like Drew had claimed? If not Penelope, someone else," Blake wondered aloud.

"I've had the same thought. If that's true, it's someone who knows the ins and outs of our business procedures and strategies." Alex's eyes sharpened as he looked at Blake. "Get our Internal Forensic Team on it stat. We need to investigate this much deeper. With so much money at stake, whoever it is would likely make a false move somewhere."

"You're thinking another employee?" Blake asked. He glanced at the waiter who placed a bowl of Manhattan clam chowder in front of him. "Thank you, Peter.

"Your favorite as usual, sir," Peter said with a smile.

Alex waited until they'd all been served and Peter had walked away before he responded. "It's possible it could be someone from the competing companies involved in the upcoming Manhattan Mall project."

"We'll start looking into that angle as well," Mark agreed. "Now mate, tell us. How did the first night go with the delightful Mrs. Carver?"

"You know a gentleman never kisses and tells," he said with a deep chuckle.

"Yeah, but since when is gentleman protocol relevant when it comes to your mates? C'mon, out with it. There's no fucking way you didn't at least have a taste of those pouty lips," Blake quipped.

Blake and Mark continued to taunt Alex but he didn't budge.

"Well, mate," Mark said with a wide smile at Blake, "That in itself speaks volumes. Alex is never shy about his sexual prowess. Wanna bet that our mate is about to fall from his throne of bachelorhood?"

"Oh, there's no doubt about that, Mark. Let's make the bet interesting and say, our friend is about to lose his heart to the enticing little brunette."

Alex snorted derisively. "Now, you've completely lost the plot, Blake. My heart is as intact as it's always been."

"Maybe for the moment, yes, but I bet you, it's not gonna stay that way. How about it, Mark, shall we say, by Christmas, Alex would not only be hitched, but he'd be smitten like a puppy."

"Go ahead, mates. I hope it's going to be a worthwhile bet. I've had my eye on that vintage Harley Davidson for a while," Alex taunted them.

"You're on! I'd love to have that lady parked in my garage, especially if I win her." Blake enthused.

"Me too. It's a bet then. If Blake is right, you get us a Harley each. If you're right, we'll get you one." Mark scrutinized Alex carefully. "Hm, I think you're right, Blake. There's a flicker in his eyes when we mention the brunette. Which color do you want?"

"Dream on. You're about to lose. Big time," Alex grunted. But he couldn't deny that his quip carried a lot less conviction than his tone expressed.

What the fuck! Get a grip, Sinclair. You're not made for marital bliss. No fucking way.

Linzi Basset

CHAPTER SIX

"I have a business to run. I can't stay cooped up in this house." Penny stabbed her finger on the counter, which reiterated her frustration. She shifted on the high barstool next to the kitchen counter, watching Alex grill steaks they were going to have for dinner. "My Fall collection is due for release soon and I'm behind with the designs as it is."

Her voice was animated, hands flailing in the air. She hated being restricted, especially when she had so much to do.

"You're a designer, Penelope. Surely you can do that anywhere? As I'm sure you have a very competent production team who can cope for the short time you're forced to stay away. Besides, it can't be helped. There has been a new development," Alex said as he basted the juicy steaks.

"What? Have you found out who Drew conspired with?"

Alex took the steaks off the grill, turned around and looked intently at her. His gaze searched beyond her eyes and reached into her soul. She felt a chill run down her back.

"You think it's me. You said you believed in my innocence two days ago. What changed?"

"The banks received a phone call this morning in an attempt to withdraw the money."

"From whom?"

"Penelope Carver."

Penny gaped at him. He reached over and pushed her chin up. She snapped her mouth shut and slapped away his hand. The gaze she shot at him was edged with the sharpness of a dagger. She dug out her phone from the back pocket of her jeans. She slid it over the counter toward him with a jerk.

"Feel free to check my call log. Or, no wait, you'll just accuse me of deleting it from the call register. Why don't you instruct Agent Farrow to dig out my caller history from my service provider—he's already done it once before."

"Look, Penelope, I want to believe you but you can't deny—"

"You know what, Sinclair? I don't give a rat's ass whether or not you believe me. I know I did nothing wrong and I'm getting fed up with the constant accusations. For that matter, I've had it with being a prisoner here." She slid from the barstool and walked toward the door leading to the hallway. "You have a beautiful home but you suck as a host. I'm leaving. I'm going home."

"Why don't you rather prove your innocence to me, Penelope?" Alex asked in an enigmatic tone.

"Why should I?"

"Because you hate that your honesty and integrity are being questioned."

Penny leaned against the door frame; her back toward him. She bit her lip, annoyed and surprised that he'd read her feelings so well. Growing up, Gran had instilled both the traits in her. She'd always thought herself an honorable person. It infuriated her that because of Drew her honor had been compromised.

She pivoted around.

"How exactly am I supposed to do that?"

"Drew's death left me with a question mark. It's put me and the integrity of my company in jeopardy."

"But you'll get the money back as soon as I've figured out the code."

"The money is of little consequence, Penelope. We have insurance to cover that, although I hope it doesn't come to that."

"If it's not about the money—"

"Drew led everyone to believe that you and he were a happily married couple, with a baby on the way."

"*What?* Why the devil would he do that?"

"Your late husband—"

"*Ex*-husband," Penny snapped.

"*Ex*-husband was a pathological liar. He weaved a web of lies to get his way. His lies have played an integral role in our partnership with Chi Fung Foundation—an extremely important redevelopment project for me and my company—but his lies have now put the whole deal in jeopardy. This is partly a charity project, aimed to rehabilitate the Chinese community in Chinatown with improved living and working conditions."

"That's very commendable. I read an article about that project in the papers."

"I do the charity, or re-development projects in honor of my mother. We didn't have much when I was growing up but she always had enough to help others. It's my way of keeping her spirit alive. What started as an ode to her memory has now become a passion and has been a very rewarding experience, enabling people for a better life. That's what this project is to me. I've already injected millions of my personal funds in the project and I will do anything to remain in the driving seat and see this project through."

"I don't understand what Drew's death has to do with that."

"To Zhang, family values are above everything else. It's why he's part of this project, contributing considerably for the oriental population of Chinatown. He was taken in by Drew and the picture of marital bliss he presented. Because Blake and I are unmarried, Zhang is leery of dealing with us. It matters to him that the person handling the project has the same values at heart. Zhang called today. They're threatening to pull the plug."

"Can they do that?"

"The contract is airtight but knowing that Drew had lied to them, leaves us in a precarious position to begin with. I need to make them see that family is just as important to us, as it is to him. It's the only way to guarantee he honors the agreement without things turning sour and ugly."

"How?"

"I need a wife."

Penny felt the earth drop. Whatever else she'd expected, *that* was the last thing she'd thought to hear. Her heart rate jumped as her mind filled with visions of being married to *this* man.

"A wife?" She managed to croak; her throat suddenly felt like she'd swallowed a ton of sand. "A real wife or a pretend wife?"

"I don't do pretend, Penelope." Alex kept his face impassive, although a shard of guilt shot through him for lying about this being a temporary arrangement.

I'll cross that bridge when I come to it.

"I didn't think so," she muttered under her breath.

"Well? What do you say?" Alex watched her steadfastly.

"Me? You want to *marry me*?"

Alex shrugged. "Two flies with one swat, luv. Marrying me would prove that you are willing to do what you can to get to the bottom of Drew's embezzlement and help me to fix the fuckup he left behind."

"I just managed to divorce one husband. What makes you think I want another?"

"Don't ever make the mistake of comparing me with Drew Carver, Penelope."

"I didn't mean . . . look, I don't want a husband. *Any* husband. You included. Period."

Alex lazily stretched to his full height and prowled around the island counter toward her. He cupped her chin with his palm and circled her neck with the other. He slowly dragged her closer, his gaze focused on her glistening lips.

"Well, then, let's see if I can change your mind, shall we?"

"I don't think—"

His lips caught hers under his, effectively cutting off her protest. His lips enveloped her, owned her. A fire ignited inside as their bodies moved together, soft curves against unyielding steel. Penny inhaled frantically, but it wasn't enough. She felt lightheaded. With a breathy sigh, she capitulated and kissed him back—with a passionate demand of her own. He responded with a groan against her mouth. It was a seriously lustful, open-mouthed kiss that shattered them both and then remade them whole. Alex groaned long and hard into her mouth.

Penny was amazed at his reaction to her. The groan was loud, feral and erotic. She knew it was a sound she would remember for a long time; how it vibrated against her lips, echoing into her mouth. A low moan escaped from deep in her throat, as hot blood coursed through her. Her skin bloomed under his touch. In her entire thirty years, she'd never experienced such a rush of arousal as she did in this kiss with Alex.

This kiss.

It was unsettling but she'd be damned if she didn't enjoy it.

"Oh," Penny cried in surprise when Alex picked her up. She tightened her arms around his neck as heated waves rocked and swayed her against the musculature of his chest.

He sat her down on the fourth step of the staircase, spread her legs, and settled between them before she could comprehend what he was about.

"You are like a prized Arabian filly, Penelope. Graceful, fiery and yet delicate," he said reverently.

She bit her lip as his hands pushed her dress over her hips. He leaned back, his eyes lingered on the toned lines of her stomach that he'd just bared. He brushed his fingers where his gaze had strayed. Her eyes flared and her breath caught in her throat. He traced the edge of the red satin panties, teasing the softness of her inner thighs.

"Your spicy bouquet has haunted me since yesterday, Penelope. Now, I get to taste."

"You . . . I . . . ohh!" She gasped as he blatantly ripped the flimsy piece of triangle from her hips. She watched it flutter down the steps. "Oooh, my lord," she moaned as he breathed hotly on her exposed flesh, his gaze intent and hungry. As if hypnotized by the vision, his fingers delved between the delicate lips and strummed her clitoris.

Softly, like the touch of a butterfly.

Teasing, testing her willingness at first and then drawing tantalizing circles around the tip.

Penny surrendered by arching her back and tilting her hips harder against his hand as shards of pleasure shot through her loins. It had been so long and the little tease of the previous morning had thoroughly whetted her appetite for more.

"You're so beautiful in your arousal, luv. Resisting you is impossible," Alex murmured, his gaze was riveted to her flushed body, undulating under his expert touch. She was tight but lubricated enough to accommodate two of his long fingers as he pushed them inside her pussy. "So hot and passionate." He pulled out his fingers to spread her essence over her clitoris, wetting it, his intent shining through his indigo eyes.

Penny held her breath as he moved lower. Her hoarse cry echoed through the house as he kissed his way over the swales of her belly. Her breathing turned choppy when his lips caressed the soft skin just where the smooth puffy folds hid her treasure. His fingers slipped back inside and he began to pump them gently in and out, ensuring his fingers grazed against the swollen ganglia inside her vagina.

"What are you *doing*? We can't . . . oh, Jesus!" Penny's protest faded as she began to lose the battle against the kisses and licks from his wicked lips.

"The feel of your satiny skin against my tongue is addictive, luv. It's time to see if you taste as good as you smell."

Penny lost the ability to think when he flicked his rogue tongue in one long lick from the back of her slit to the top, ending with a teasing stab against her clit. With the fourth pass of his tongue, the urge to resist dissipated completely. Her legs spread wider and hips surged higher in a silent offering.

"Ah, thanks, luv," he acknowledged her plea. "Now, I can feast all I want."

He growled as he spread her pussy lips and pushed his marauding tongue deep inside her pussy. He probed deep with swirling motions before he sensually licked and sucked the silky folds, boldly quenching his desire.

Penny was mindless to the hard, uncomfortable stairs beneath her. All that mattered was Alex, his magical touch and his *very industrious* mouth.

Oh god!

"That feels so good," she wailed as he feasted on her pussy with the fervor of a dying man enjoying his last meal.

Alex drifted on the same cloud as her, intoxicated by her scent and the taste of her honeyed juices.

"Now *this* I can easily do all-night long," he drawled against her quivering flesh. He pushed her legs wider and pulled her labia open with his fingers. "*Fuck,* what a beautiful sight," he groaned as he pushed his mouth hard into her slit, probing even deeper than before. He moved his face back and forth, his nose teasing the edge of her clit. His eyes, however, were fixed on her rapturous face.

Penny moaned nonstop and then with a husky scream, she erupted in an orgasm strong enough to move the earth for her.

"Yes, Penelope, give it to me," Alex encouraged against her labia, feverishly lapping and sucking her clit as he plunged two fingers inside her. He continued to thrust his hand into her with a hard, sensual rhythm that his body demanded from him. He watched her face, her eyes. He was entranced by the emotions that flashed there.

Penny bucked and thrashed against his mouth as he mercilessly gorged on her pussy, drawing another climax from her.

"Oh god! Oh god," she choked out, finding it hard to draw a proper breath.

Alex relented and eased up, rubbing her labia and buttocks, letting her body relax.

"Please, Alex," she said with wheezing breath. The desire to feel his hard cock driving into her was all consuming.

He didn't have to ask what she was after. It was there in her expression, in the tautness of her body. A demand that his own body was screaming out to him. He resolutely pushed his own desire down.

"Will you marry me, Penelope?"

Penny's state of arousal was so high that she struggled to comprehend what he was asking and then to formulate the words to respond.

"I told you, I don't—"

"Hm . . . it seems I've got my work cut out for me."

His gaze was enigmatic as their eyes met. He exulted in the flare of her eyes, the little catch of her breath when he stroked her thighs. He watched as his fingers brush over her wet labia once again. Her moans turned to soft wailing sounds as he flicked his fingers over her clit with renewed fervor, intent on getting the answer that he wanted.

He slipped a finger inside her scorching pussy.

Then two.

Then three.

A flush darkened his cheeks as he watched her labia spread wide enough to accommodate his girth. *Hopefully.*

"Please, I need . . . I need . . . aahh," Penny cried out and bowed her back as Alex pounded his hand into her, making her braless breasts jiggle underneath her dress. It was a mesmerizing sight for Alex.

"Yes, you do, luv," he said feverishly. He sucked the swollen nub of her clit into his mouth. "Gorgeous and such a succulent little treasure," he moaned as his tongue thrilled against the tip. He watched her carefully, bringing her to the precipice of another climax. And holding her there.

"I'm afraid, Penelope, until you give me what I want, my cock won't come anywhere near this juicy pussy of yours."

Having said that, he redoubled his efforts; thrusting his fingers deeper, harder into her sopping pussy. Penny panted and moaned incessantly as he curled his fingers inward and brushed his fingertips against the swollen nub inside. She thrashed and canted her hips against his mouth.

"God! *Please!*" Her back arched as she desperately humped his hand, fervently chasing the elusive pleasure that he ruthlessly kept feeding.

Alex was inflamed by her passionate response. His cock pulsed and throbbed with need. He couldn't remember the last time he had been *this* aroused by a woman.

"Please, please, Alex," she whimpered.

Alex came up to place soft, nibbling kisses on her lips. His breath was warm against her temple. His voice was laced with his own raging arousal as he whispered, "It's late, luv. Best we finish dinner, so you can go to bed."

And then, he was gone. Penny didn't move. *She couldn't.* She struggled to regulate her breathing. Her stomach rolled in waves of lustful need that still coursed through her. Talk about getting shafted royally—or in this case, *not.* She was splayed open on the stairs. Every cell in her body sizzled with desire.

"You're a fucking *asshole*, Alexander Sinclair," she managed to squeak through clenched teeth.

His chuckle echoed back to her from the kitchen.

"Believe me, luv, I've been called much worse."

CHAPTER SEVEN

"It's all your fault. And you call yourself my best friend? Gmphf! *Traitor* is more like it." Penny rolled her eyes, accusing Amber. She made wide circles with the knife in her hand, about to pontificate further.

"Now that's not fair," Amber preempted her. "All I did was look out for you."

"By handing me to a wolf in sheep's clothing!"

"Come now, Penny, think about it. It goes to reason that Drew's co-conspirator would know all about you *and* your best friend. Therefore, it's the first place they would come looking for you."

"I guess you're right," Penny admitted grudgingly. "It's just . . . he's so . . . he's a fucking asshole!"

Alex's car had just disappeared through the front gate of his property when Penny had phoned a cab to pick her up. She was aware of the protective detail around the house, so she had no doubt that they had followed her to Amber's restaurant. Of course, *he* would also know by now that she'd ignored his explicit order to *stay indoors.*

She'd gone to her office to work on her designs but had given up an hour later. After every drawing ended in the trash, there had only been one place to go.

"No! Put down those zucchinis, Penelope. It's too early to start chopping them. We're still serving breakfast, for goodness sake!" Amber grabbed the container out of her hands and placed it out of her reach. "From the agonized expression on your face, I'm guessing that your Mr. Sinclair hasn't satisfied your back-from-dead ovaries yet."

Penny slanted a heated glance at Amber. She threw her hands in the air and stomped toward Amber's office, leaving her no choice but to follow.

"I don't know myself anymore, Amber," Penny said as she slumped into the chair. "That man has me tied up in knots. I feel like a silly school girl. Shit! I'm acting like one too. Where is the calm, cool and collected Penelope Winters?"

"Winters?"

"Yes, I received the confirmation this morning that my surname has officially been reinstated. If not for this mess Drew has gotten me into, I would've celebrated being rid of Carver for good."

"Does the FBI have a plan to get you out of it?"

"I wish. I doubt any of them truly believe I'm innocent."

"That's hogwash! Didn't they do a proper background check on you . . . or the history between you and that bastard?"

"Yes, but Drew misled everyone to believe that we were a poster of suburban happiness. What doesn't help is the fact that a woman phoned the offshore banks yesterday claiming to be me." Penny shrugged. "I suppose they'll verify my caller history with my service provider but it's just so debilitating, you know? That my word and honor are doubted."

"I can imagine how you must feel. Does Alex believe you?"

"He says he wants to but I think he has doubts." Penny turned pensive. "Which makes me wonder why he's so *hell-bent* on marrying me?"

Amber choked in surprise. "Whoa! Back up there, Penelope Winters! *Marry you*? When did that happen?"

Penny briefly told Amber what had led to the unexpected marriage proposal, albeit an abridged version.

"On the stairs? Well, you go girl!"

"*That's* what you got from that?" Penny asked with a grin that belied the rosy tint of embarrassment on her cheeks.

"Well damn, it sounds like your sex life is about to become very entertaining," Amber defended herself. "Face it. Neither of us have had any excitement in the bedroom of late. At least listening to your risqué encounter gives me hope!"

"I find it difficult to believe that you don't have a line-up of men to service your needs, Blondie," Blake's deep voice drawled from the doorway.

Penny was intrigued by the blush that immediately bloomed over Amber's cheeks as her gaze got caught by Blake's.

Penny glanced over her shoulder. "Ugh! What are *you* doing here? Can't you leave me alone for even one day?"

"You're the one begging for my attention all the time, sweetheart." Alex gestured around. "This isn't where I told you to stay when I left the house?"

Penny crossed her arms defiantly. "You aren't the boss of me and besides, I'll go batshit crazy if I stay cooped up in that house one more day. I told you, I have a company to run."

"Hmm, which poses the question, what are you doing here?" Alex prodded with an amused tone.

"I don't have to explain my movements to you, Sinclair."

"Very well." Alex took out his phone and made a call. His voice was clipped, with a dark edge in the sudden silence of the room. "Mark, it's time to take Penelope Winters into custody."

"What?"

"What?!"

Penny and Amber's simultaneous cries drowned Alex's voice. Penny twisted in her chair to stare at him, shock apparent on her face.

"You're not serious," she raged at him.

His eyes bored into hers with an enigmatic expression on his face as he continued unperturbed, "Yes, Mark. She's done nothing to win my confidence. I'm not sure if she's as innocent as she claims to be. I believe it will be better to keep her behind bars until we get to the truth. She's undependable—"

"Okay! God, I hate you," Penny snapped. Her body shuddered with anger. "Just what do you want from me?"

"Put a hold on that arrest for now, Mark. I'll get back to you." Alex returned the phone to his pocket. With an unrepentant grin on his face, he leaned closer to growl softly into Penny's ear, "You know what I want, Penelope."

"That's nothing short of blackmail!" Penny retorted; her expression belligerent.

"That's a matter of opinion. I'd prefer to call it *persuasion*." Alex looked at Blake. "We might as well

109

have breakfast here." He pinned Penny with a piercing look. "Seeing as the one at the office was interrupted."

"Gmphf!" Penny responded as she offered him her back.

"Perfect. I'm *starving*." Blake grinned at Amber, which brought another flush to her cheeks at the emphasis he placed on the last word, accompanied by a sardonic lift of his eyebrows. The double entendre wasn't even subtle.

Alex turned to leave. "We expect you ladies to join us."

"Now look here, Sinclair. You might believe you have the right to order me around but leave Amber out of this," Penny hissed with irritation laced in every word.

Alex grinned engagingly at Amber over his shoulder. "We'd be delighted to have your company for breakfast, Ms. Summers."

"Don't mind if I do." Amber smiled at him while doing her best to ignore the gorgeous man to his right. It seemed that he couldn't take his eyes off her.

Penny gaped at her, ignoring the two men disappearing down the hallway.

"I don't believe you, Amber Summers! Don't you see what he's doing?"

"Inviting me to breakfast has an ulterior motive?"

"He's aiming to use your influence to sway me. Just like he did three days ago!"

"Penny, I've known you for as long as I can remember. You have never in all these years allowed anyone to bully you into anything. Not consciously. You're an over thinker. You know that, as well as I do. You'll make your decision, just as you did when you went home with Alex. Come on, admit it," Amber dared her as she took off her chef's jacket and pulled the scrunchy from her blonde hair. She shook loose the long silky tresses that fell over her shoulders.

"You know what to do, Penny."

"You have more confidence in my abilities than I do at this stage, Amber."

"Come on, girl. What do you always do when faced with a difficult decision?"

"Weigh up the pros and cons."

"Exactly. But let me caution you. Don't allow a false sense of responsibility for Drew's fuckups sway you into making the wrong choice."

"That's exactly what worries me."

"Then start there. You don't owe Drew's memory shit! Not a goddamned thing; so, eliminate him from the equation straight away."

"What else is there, Amber? The bottom line is I don't *owe* Alexander Sinclair any loyalty either."

"I sense a *but*," Amber prodded instinctively. She knew Penny too well not to know what was behind her indecision. Now, it was up to Penny to realize it herself.

Penny inhaled deeply. "There shouldn't be one," she bemoaned her confusion.

"But you can't just walk away from him."

"Ahh! Curse my ovaries!" she wailed.

Amber laughed. "You can deny it all you want, Penny but there's more than just chemistry that you feel for Alex. And no, it's not just your libido. I believe his reasons for insisting on marrying you are suspect."

"You think so?"

"Think about it, girl! Why push you for the real thing when he could get away with a pretend marriage?"

Penny stared at her. It had never crossed her mind. Not once during the long hours of the night when she'd stayed awake pondering over Alex's unexpected proposal. The thought of being Alex's wife wasn't unexciting. For one thing, marriage to him would be a lot more satisfying than it had been with Drew. All night she'd been trying to convince herself why she *shouldn't* accept his proposal. But she's never questioned why he needed one in the first place.

"It's ludicrous, Amber. I don't know the man from a bar of soap. We only met three days ago, for heaven's sake."

Amber smiled softly as she stared at Penny. What she wouldn't give to be in Penny's shoes.

"You should count your blessings, Penny. Not everyone is lucky enough to get second chances. Things may not have turned out great with Drew, but here you have another chance of finding happiness. I don't know Alex much, but from what I've read about him, I believe that he's an honorable man. It's really hard to find one of those in New York City, my friend and nothing to scoff at."

"I'm not scoffing . . . I just . . . after Drew, I don't trust my judgment implicitly. And I don't want to get hurt, Amber. Not again."

"I understand that, Penny but use the weapons at your disposal. He might be citing all kinds of reasons for the proposed wedding but you can change the outcome, girlfriend."

Penny pondered what Amber was saying. Hope began to flicker in the depths of her heart. She didn't understand the attraction she felt for Alex. All she knew was that she was a moth to his flame, and combustion was inevitable.

"Humans have an infinite capacity to love, Penny. Circumstances may make you question your feelings, but you should be open to possibilities. That's how miracles happen, sweetie. Dig deep inside your own soul. You know what's waiting to burst to the surface. Use that and make him yours."

"Yeah, you seem to forget we're talking about the formidable Alexander Sinclair."

"Maybe, but he's a human first, with a heart and a soul. I know you don't believe in love at first sight but somehow, this time you're smack in the middle of your own fairytale and don't even know it, Sleeping Beauty. Grasp what life is offering you with both hands, Penny. This time it will be your choice."

"You're right. Love and be loved. That's what I've always wanted. Very well, girlfriend. Tonight, I'm making that pros and cons list."

"That's the spirit. Now, shall we?" Amber ambled toward the door.

"I thought you already had breakfast," Penny quipped as they made their way to the dining room.

"I could do with some blueberry pancakes. Besides," she winked at Penny, "he offered me a ringside seat to the best show I'll be seeing in a long time. I should bring some PornCoc to munch on—oops . . . I meant popcorn," she joked, tongue-in-cheek.

Amber giggled, "Of course. I don't suppose the muscle-palace with Alex has anything to do with your sudden craving for pancakes?"

Another telltale blush colored Amber's cheeks.

"I'm not sure what you're talking about."

"In that case, I need a giant bucket of . . . what did you call it? Ah yes. *PornCoc!*" Penny's tinkling laughter lasted all the way to the table.

Her melodious laughter was like a pebble making ripples in a still pond. It radiated outward through the packed dining room to reach inside his mind. Alex wouldn't be surprised if even the birds stopped chirping to listen to the beautiful sound emerging from her pouty lips. It filled the air with a husky sensuality; a composition that could very well become his favorite song.

His expression was enigmatic as he watched her approach. For the first time since they'd met, she was completely relaxed. The mirth in her eyes and the bubbling smile on her lips held his gaze mesmerized. The realization, that he *wanted* to be the reason for her smile, shook him.

"So, mate, what's the real reason for asking Penny to marry you?" Blake prodded as he examined the impassive expression on his friend's face.

A vertical line drew Alex's brows together. *What? I'd be fucked if I knew myself.*

For one thing, why hadn't he told Penelope that it would be a temporary arrangement? It seems his common sense had taken a sabbatical since the moment he laid eyes on her and her pouty lips.

Alex had never had the desire to get hitched. He didn't believe in love and he didn't trust easily, not after watching his mother suffer. For that matter, he didn't even *know* how to love. In his thirty-six years of existence, he'd slept and had sex with more women than he cared to admit. Not once had his heart been in it. It just wasn't in his DNA. Maybe he was more like his father than he was willing to acknowledge.

He didn't expect his heart to be involved this time either.

Yeah, if that's the truth, then why the fuck are you forcing Penelope to marry you?

"You know me, Blake," he hedged dryly.

Blake chuckled. "Yeah, sure. But you forget that I know you better than you do yourself. And, no, Alex, I'm not referring to your testosterone.

Lusting after her is a no-brainer. But you, my friend, want more from her. All of her. Period."

"You're delusional."

"Am I?" He laughed again. "Mark and I should go and place our orders for those Harleys this weekend."

"Harleys? As in Harley Davidson?" Penny's eyes sparkled with interest as she and Amber joined them and sat down.

"You like motorcycles?" Alex was increasingly surprised by the puzzle that was, Penelope Winters, as the days went past.

"I love them. When I was little, I went to rallies with my parents every weekend," she enthused.

"She more than loves them. She's a rider too," Amber volunteered.

"Well, that's a surprise. A little sprite like you handling an eight-hundred-pound machine? That, I'd like to see." There was open admiration in Alex's voice.

Penny laughed. "I own a vintage—it was my mother's bike and I've maintained it for the past twenty years. It's a 1985 Harley Davidson FatBoy; it suits my short height and is much lighter."

"Sandy has been your baby girl for years and you know it," Amber quipped.

"Yes, that's true and she's a little jealous of Hades," Penny laughed in agreement.

"Hades?" Alex was taken by the excitement in her eyes.

"Yes, my Sportster-1200-Nightster. I bought it as a celebratory gift for myself when Drew finally signed the divorce papers."

"I'll be damned."

Penny gazed Alex mockingly. "Good, it'll save me the trouble."

"Careful, luv, you're talking about my future wife's husband," he taunted her with a crooked smile.

Penny's lips flattened into a line. "I'll stay for breakfast on the condition that the topic of marriage or Drew Carver doesn't come up."

"Hallelujah! Give the girl a gold star," Blake applauded her. He turned to Amber and grasped her hand in his. His thumb drew slow circles on her palm as he gazed into her eyes. "Blake Harper, at your pleasure, Blondie."

"Amber." She yanked her hand from his. "My name is *Amber* and you can spare me the cheesy flirting routine."

Blake glanced at Alex with amusement on his face. "It seems we've got two fiery ones on our hands, mate."

"Really? On your hands? Does that kind of thing usually work for you?" Penny asked dryly, which drew a deep chuckle from Alex. It did funny things to certain of her body parts. That mouth though . . .

Alex's gaze sharpened as he watched Penny's eyes glaze at the memory. He breached her private space to graze his lips over the scallop of her ear. He noticed the answering shudder of her body as he whispered, "Careful, luv, I have a feeling you're starting to like me."

"That's a classic case of wishful thinking, Sinclair."

"That sounds like a challenge, sweetie. You should know that I thrive on that."

"I wasn't—"

"Challenge accepted." He breathed hotly in her ear. "Brace yourself, Penelope. You don't stand a chance against what's coming."

"Shall we get you two a room?" Blake drawled.

Penny felt her face suffuse with heat, but Alex took his sweet time before drawing back from her. She was shocked at how cold she felt without his hard body pressed against her. It was a chill that coursed through her entire being, leaving her feeling shaken and fragile.

Alarm bells went off in her mind. What Amber had said came rushing to the surface of her mind. She couldn't deny that she lusted after Alex but the prospect of being his sole focus intimidated her.

Their eyes met in a smoldering moment that caught them both unawares. Something magical happened between them in that split second of realization. The air around them crackled with electricity.

Alex was startled at first, until he read the reciprocal on Penny's face. It was there, as bold as the sun was shining outside.

That does it.

Her fate was sealed.

Penelope Winters was about to become Alexander Sinclair's claimed bride.

Her consent would be an added bonus but nothing was going to stand between Alex and what he wanted—to make Penelope Winters his.

In every way.

Come hell or high water.

Chapter Eight

"Good morning, I'm Gabrielle Brittle, inside counsel for the Allied Group. Is it a convenient time for you to talk, Mrs. Carver?"

"It's Ms. Winters. I reverted back to my maiden name," Penny corrected her automatically. "What is this about, Ms. Brittle?"

"It's in regard to the company's life insurance policy of Mr. Carver. As you know, you are the sole beneficiary of the policy. Would it be possible for you to come to my office to finalize the necessary paperwork?"

Penny stopped working on the design she was busy with. The pencil did a rat-a-tat on her desk. She'd won the battle with Alex but had to contend with the two bodyguards that followed her everywhere. She sat back with a frown.

"I'm confused. I already informed the HR Head, Dave Clinton, that I have no interest in that policy."

Silence followed Penny's terse statement. Her frown deepened. "Ms. Brittle?"

"Of course, Ms. Winters," she said in rushed voice. "However, I still require you to process the paperwork. You *do* understand? Where money is concerned, there are always legal implications if the correct procedures aren't followed. It's my responsibility to ensure that the Allied Group is protected in situations like these."

Penny was thoroughly confused. Dave Clinton had implied that he would send the necessary documentation with Alex for her to sign. A thought crossed her mind that caused a slow anger to unfurl inside her.

Did that mean that Alex somehow still didn't believe in her innocence? That she wasn't sincere when she'd insisted that Drew's life insurance policy be ceded over to the company instead? Was this a test? Why else would the company attorney suddenly be involved in this issue?

"Of course," she said; her voice was edged with a sharp chill. It didn't escape Gabrielle's notice on the other end. "When do you need me to be there?"

"The sooner, the better, Ms. Winters. I'm sure you'd prefer to put the unpleasantness behind you."

The implication was crystal clear. Alex had told her the entire sordid tale. It cemented Penny's suspicion that he *still* didn't trust her. It hurt more than she cared to admit.

"Very well. Please text me your office address. I'll let you know when I can come around."

Penny abruptly ended the connection. She returned to the design she had been working on, deliberately shutting down her mind and forced herself to stop thinking. Her movements were mechanical, sharp and precise, a reflection of the silent anger she was trying very hard to suppress. It didn't last very long. She knew she was wasting her time, since she wasn't concentrating. She blinked and the drawing she'd just finished came into focus.

"*Fuck me*," she puffed in a hushed voice.

She stared in amazed wonder at the intricate design, the flowing lines and the beauty of the drawing.

A wedding dress.

Penny shook her head as her thoughts returned to the telephone conversation.

"What is he doing? Is this another trick to force me to capitulate to his demands; to slowly chip away my peace of mind with his continuous mistrust?"

She slammed her palm on the desk. The porcelain cup, still half filled with cold tea, clattered in the saucer.

"Does he honestly think I'll marry him just to prove that I *can* be trusted?"

She frowned as she replayed the conversation in her mind. Alex was straightforward—had been from the first moment they'd met. It didn't add up with how he'd been with her since that breakfast at Amber's Cuisine. He'd started wooing her, gone out of his way to spoil her with flowers and little—inconsequential but thoughtful—gifts, in a true old-fashioned courtship. It was sweet and the effort he'd put into it had endeared him to her. Especially with the added excitement of his passionate kisses when he wished her goodnight.

If Penny had to be completely honest with herself, she was on the verge of folding. Her resistance had been crumbling and she had no doubt that Alex was aware of that.

"No, he wouldn't suddenly switch gears. Dave Clinton and Gabrielle Brittle must have their wires crossed."

She picked up the drawing and stared at it. It was a beautiful dress. The wedding dress she'd been dreaming of since she'd been a little girl. She never had the opportunity to wear one with Drew, because they had been married in Gran's hospital room.

She traced a finger over the flowing skirt of the design. It was a classic wedding gown, yet timelessly elegant, but taken to a new level. It was a sleek ivory silk sheath dress with a diaphanous chiffon and tulle overlay at the waist. She'd drawn some intricate beading and embroidery into the sketch. The illusion sweetheart neckline was delicious; designed for a killer décolletage, and was set off by the sumptuous Chantilly lace that would adorn the delicate long lace sleeves in a serpentine pattern. The long, detachable chiffon trail added to the old-world charm of the dress. The corseted bodice added an extra touch of allure, complemented by the low, open back.

Penny sighed heavily. She opened her notebook and studied the pros and cons list she'd been working on for the past three days. Not that she needed to. She already knew the answer, and no matter how many negatives she added to the list, there were three *really* good positives.

"The biggest negative, Penelope Winters, is that after the debacle with Drew you made a vow to not marry again; not unless you are one-hundred percent certain the man is the love of your life and the feeling is reciprocated."

She tapped her fingers on the desk. "That alone should negate all the positives," she mumbled.

A vision flashed in her mind, which sent a rush of heat through her body and set her skin tingling. Alex's kisses had that effect on her, not to mention, she had to walk up and down the damned stairs every day and be reminded of their scorching encounter. How effortlessly he'd molded her body and desires to his tune.

God knows, she ached for Alexander Sinclair. *Inside her body.* Possessing and taking her to heights previously unknown to her.

"And right there is a huge plus," she bemoaned her fate, choosing to ignore the fact that it was the something she could get without the benefit of marriage. She rubbed her forehead. She became more confused every time she thought about it.

Alex was different from any other man she'd ever met. He was *all* man, in every aspect of the word. Maybe that's why Penny found it so difficult to resist him—that magnetism just kept pulling her toward him, without any conscious thought from her.

But, in all honesty, like Amber had said, it was more than just physical attraction. Alex had gotten under her skin. Worse. He'd managed to squeeze past the wall she'd build around her heart in a very short period of time. There was no denying it any longer.

It felt good.

It felt *right.*

"Oh, lordy me. I've already made a decision without realizing it."

Her gaze returned to the drawing in front of her.

"Maybe my stupid heart has decided yes, but why do I feel that I'm about to tango with the *devil.*"

Penny hummed as she poured the zingy, Thai marinade over the salmon steaks and covered the dish. She enjoyed cooking but doing it for one person didn't offer the same pleasure as watching someone appreciate her efforts. She glanced at the clock as she started blanching the vegetables to ensure everything would be ready by the time Alex arrived home. He'd texted her that he was on his way ten minutes ago. Like he had been doing every day since he'd brought her here.

He was a very considerate man, something she appreciated. She felt lighthearted, relaxed and looked forward to spending time in his company. Being happy was finally an option, for the first time in years. Having made her decision, her spirits lifted to a different dimension.

"Oh," Penny gasped at warm lips pressed against the nape of her neck, followed by a pair of muscular arms wrapping around her waist, pulling her closer against his hard body.

"Evening, luv," Alex murmured against her skin. A delighted trail of goosebumps followed his fingertips over her arms. Turning her head toward him, he kissed her slowly in a meshing of warmth, passion and desire; a desire that he had stopped fighting.

Penny turned in his arms. Her hands came to rest against his chest. Unhurriedly, his fingers outlined the shape of her mouth, admiring the exquisite pulpiness of their bow shape. His touch was feathery.

"You look good enough to eat, luv." His voice was soft, as were the motions of his fingers. Dressed in skinny jeans and a red silk blouse that draped attractively over her enticing body, she brought his carnal senses to life.

Penny silently returned his heated stare, wishing, not for the first time, that she could decipher his expression. She inhaled slowly to gather her confidence.

"Yes."

One word.

Such a simple one but it impacted like a cannonball, directly at Alex's heart. He didn't ask what she meant. Her eyes said it all. He cupped her cheeks between his palms. His eyes turned warm as he stared into hers. His lips came within a fraction of hers.

"*Yes.*"

His voice deepened as he captured her sigh with a kiss. Their breaths mingled. He claimed her quivering lips with a hunger that shook her. Penny's arms wrapped around his neck as he swept her off her feet. She returned the kiss with equal fervor. The kiss deepened. His hands explored the rounded curve of her buttocks as he brought her tighter against him.

Alex ended the kiss reluctantly. He closed his eyes and held her, allowing her essence to flow unchecked through him. He switched off the stove, picked her up and strode toward the stairs.

"Alex," she breathed, pointing toward the kitchen. "Our dinner—"

"Can wait. My desire for you—can't. It's been hell keeping my hands off you."

Alex didn't have the patience for slow, seductive undressing and made short work of their clothes when they arrived in the room.

"Alex, I . . . ooh!" she exclaimed when he tumbled her onto her back on the bed. His warm body settled between her legs as he tangled his fingers with hers, pressing them against the mattress. Penny battled to breathe as his searing body covered her already heated skin. His weight on her felt divine.

129

"Do you have any idea how much I want you, Penelope?"

His rich voice flowed through her, eliciting a tremor of excitement inside her loins. Her clitoris started throbbing when he slowly pushed apart her legs with his knees. He smiled crookedly as he noticed her eyes flare when he pressed his tumescent cock hard against the softness of her heated core.

Penny sighed as his warm lips trailed tender kisses on the inside of her arm, slowly dragging his tongue downward, to place soft kisses on the rounded curve of her breast.

"So beautiful," he praised as he discovered the soft slopes of her breasts with his fingers. He traced the globe while kissing a slow path on the underside of the other. Teasingly, aiming closer to the tip, he watched intently as the nub slowly turned taut. His mouth preyed leisurely over the skin of her neck and shoulders.

Licking . . .

Tasting . . .

Nibbling . . .

Biting . . .

He set millions of her nerve endings abuzz and clamoring for more.

"And responsive," he murmured with his lips a mere inch from the aching tips, blowing his hot breath in an enticing promise of what was to come.

Penny was overwhelmed with unknown emotions as he laid her bare to sensations she never knew existed. It awakened a wantonness that had her arching her back as she offered her bounty as a sacrifice to him. She was thrilled at the sensual heat that he exuded. At the same time, it frightened her. This man could make her dance like a marionette in his arms.

"Hmmm," Penny moaned, her body arched into his tongue when he teased the tip with languid laving motions. "Yess," she sighed as he brushed his palm with feathery lightness over the other. He continued the barely-there touch, alternately touching and licking from the one nipple to the other, deliberately ignoring the silent writhing demand of Penny's body.

"Tell me what you want, luv," he prodded with his lips hovering over a taut nipple.

"Please, Alex. You know what I want," she breathed out in desperation.

"Ah yes, I guess I do but I want to hear you say it, Penelope," he said, loving the feel of her tight body beneath his.

She arched her back higher, desperate to feel his wicked mouth surrounding the aching tips.

"I need to feel your heat. Suck them. Please," she begged.

"I love to hear you beg me, luv," he growled in a deep voice. The torture continued for a moment longer, before, with a salacious lick, he pulled the nub deep into his mouth, sucking on it with long, deep motions—pulling it upward.

Penny mewled like a kitten when he suckled her nipples like a starving man for endless minutes. She protested in a breathy whimper when he released the nipple with a pop and began to kiss his way lower, to end in a foray of licks—up and down—on the inside of her thighs. Penny jerked when he nibbled at the tasty confluence of flesh that joined her hips and pelvis. Her breath caught in her throat, shocked to the core by the incinerating heat inside of her loins, before it surged upward to consume her whole.

Alex traced his tongue along her pelvic bone, leaving an iridescent trail of saliva behind. He brushed her soft, smooth labia before slowly inserting a long finger inside—exploring, twisting and probing deeper, all the while watching her face twist with increasing pleasure.

"More," Penny hissed as she raised her hips and orbited against his devilish mouth. She was swamped by a sudden desperation to feel his tongue and lips taste her. It was a heady feeling, to be this aroused, this *needy*. She fisted her hand in his hair and guided his mouth to where she needed him the most. Her entire body felt like it was on fire. Every cell in her body thrummed as she twisted and turned beneath him, completely subsumed in a wave of unbridled lust.

"Easy there, luv," he admonished with a gentle smile. He drew back, pushed her legs wider and slid two fingers inside her. He began to pump and twist his hand, searching, feeling for the spongy flesh on the front wall of her vagina. Penny whimpered as intense shocks of pleasure wracked her body as he scored her nerve endings over and over again.

"Oh lord, *that feels so good,*" she hissed. She pushed her head into the pillow, her mouth opening in rapture as he brushed and caressed her sweet spot; pushing and tapping against it with ruthless precision. Penny was helpless against his onslaught. She orbited her pelvis in tight circles, unconsciously thrusting her hips into his imbedded fingers.

Her face flushed, she begged with desperation quivering in her voice, "I need you inside me, Alex," she moaned with a breathy voice.

"Almost there, luv. Almost," he hissed as he leaned closer. A stuttering sob escaped from Penny's throat as his lips closed around her clit.

"Good god, Alex!" she shouted. She clamped her legs around his head, holding him prisoner against her pussy as she bucked wildly onto his hand and mouth. With a salacious hunger, he sucked the swollen nub deep into his mouth, swirling his tongue over the tip. Penny cried out in the throes of euphoria, helpless as a rush of heat flooded her before a clear discharge coated his fingers.

She was still in the midst of the climax when Alex pushed his engorged cock inside her, just an inch. He stopped to study her face.

"I'm clean, Penelope. Do you want me to wear a condom? I have to admit, I've never wanted to feel a woman's heat against my skin as I do yours."

"I'm on the pill," Penny puffed, ignoring the little voice that warned her that she'd been forgetful in taking them more often than not lately.

He flexed inside of her, grimacing at the tight heat that beckoned him like a siren.

"Oh lord, yes!" She grinded her teeth as she writhed in a paroxysm of ecstasy. His hard heat was almost more than she could bear.

"You are so fucking beautiful in your arousal," Alex said as he caught her open mouth with his. He plunged his tongue in and then nibbled on her lower lip.

"Absolutely, unbelievably sensual," he murmured, his breath exploded from his lips in short hot bursts. She wailed as he pushed all the way inside her in one ruthless sweep and started to pound her with ragged thrusts, already on the brink of losing the tight hold he had over his control.

Penny wrapped her legs high around his waist, tilting her hips, to force his cock in to the hilt.

"Yes, hell, yes!" She gulped as he continued to plunge his velvety shaft deep inside her with long rhythmic strokes. Penny's heart raced, her mind floundered with the emotions at war with her senses. She was filled to the brink; every thrust mingled his taut flesh with the swollen synaptic nerves deep inside her. Her loins tightened with painful intensity, drawing a low moan from her.

"Alex, I need . . . oohh! I need . . ."

She bit her lip when he increased the tempo of his pumping his hips; the slapping sound of his skin against her clitoris, ringing in her ears.

"Oh fuck!" she shrieked, as he continued to bang her relentlessly.

"Yes, Penelope. This is what I want. Your complete capitulation," Alex said through clenched teeth. Her tight, fleshy sheath began to spasm around him. "Ah fuck, you're so tight," he moaned. He plunged deeper into her, pillaging her softness as he tilted her hips even higher to pound her mercilessly. Reaching between their bodies, he found her clitoris and tapped it with wicked intent.

"Alex!" Penny's hoarse scream further incited his insatiable lust.

"Yes, baby. Give it to me. Give me *everything* you've got," he grunted in a raw, animal-like sound. He dragged a ragged breath into his lungs while he tried to control his precipitous fervor.

"*Hot damn*, Penelope, you feel so good."

Alex could've sworn in that moment that he'd never experienced a tenth of the pleasure with any of the other women in his life. It felt right. He felt complete.

She made him feel complete.

He leaned down to kiss her lips. He finally lost the battle to keep himself in check. His breathing became choppy as he was consumed by her passion. His cock swelled even more inside her silky walls, flinging her circuitry into overload as he drove into her with wild, uncontrolled strength. It flung her so high; it left her floating in a sphere of euphoria, before it submerged her with explosions of pleasure.

"Ohh! Oh god, oh god," she wailed, her eyes rolled upward as she gave in to him, unable to do anything but clamp her legs around him as he wrung spasm after spasm from her body.

Alex watched her expression contort with bliss as he felt her pussy clench uncontrollably around him. It flung him into a need so high, he lost control of himself. He powered into her, desperate to reach the same level of pleasure that wracked her helpless body.

Heat exploded in his head and spread with a delicious wave of fire through his body. His brain shut down. Every breath, every sensory and every source of energy was now concentrated on his release, as he ejaculated deep inside her.

"*Jesus*, Penelope," he breathed and slumped on top of her, their ragged breathing mingling in a harmony of shared bliss.

He fisted his hand around a clump of her hair, holding her in place for a quick, hard kiss. His eyes searched hers with such intensity that her breath caught in her throat.

"Now, there's no turning back, luv. From this moment forth, you are mine. *Only mine.*"

Penny was still reeling from the possessive glint in his eyes when two loud cracks of his palm landed on her buttocks, echoing through the room.

"Ooww!" She shrieked and scrambled backward on the bed. She scorched him with an accusing look. "What was that for?" She demanded crossly as she rubbed her burning behind.

"Feed me, woman. I'm starving."

"You're the one who . . ."

Her narrowing eyes were a contradiction to the sensual smile that curved around her lips. She straightened and got off the bed and started walking toward the door with gently swaying hips.

Alex found his eyes glued to the two bright spots on the enticing, rounded globes disappearing through the door.

"Where are you going, luv?"

"Why, babe, to finish dinner, like you ordered." Her sultry voice floated back to him from the hallway.

"Penelope, you're buck naked," he shouted after her.

"Brilliant deduction, Sinclair." Her tingling laughter thrilled him. "I've always wanted to have sex in the kitchen."

You're so screwed, Sinclair.

Needless to say, Alex's hunger for food was only appeased later.

Much later.

Claimed Bride

CHAPTER NINE

"You don't have to take me out to dinner so often, Alex. I'm happy to cook for us at home," Penny said as she took the seat he held out for her. She glanced coyly at him. "Or, is it your subtle way of letting me know that my cooking sucks?"

Alex sat down. "You're an excellent cook, luv and you know that very well." He took her hand and brought it to his lips. "I love to show off my gorgeous future wife to the world, Penelope. Don't deny me the pleasure."

His deep voice affected her like it always did, leaving her breathless. Penny couldn't curb the thrill of excitement his words brought to bear. Irrespective of the reasons they were getting married, since she'd agreed to his proposal, he'd been treating her like a queen. She basked in it and it showed her glowing face.

"I asked Blake, Mark and Amber to join us. I hope you don't mind?"

"Of course not." She took a gulp of the wine the server had just poured. "Talking about Mark, has the FBI found anything new about Drew's co-conspirator?"

"Nothing. Whoever it was, played their cards very close to their chest. Apart from the missing five-million-dollars, at face value, everything points to Drew as the sole culprit."

"I've been wracking my mind but I honestly have no idea what code he could've possibly used. If only I knew what it consisted of. You know, a combination of letters and figures, and how many, maybe then I'd be able to figure it out. The sooner the money is back where it belongs, the sooner my life can return to normal. I hate having shadows following me around all the time."

"I'd much rather keep you out of the line of fire, Penelope. Mark and I are going to use our influence to find a way to recover the money. Our teams are gathering all the traces they can to prove that he stole the money from the company. If we provide proof to the authorities in the US, they can compel the banks to turn the funds over to us."

"Does that mean you truly believe that I had nothing to do with it?"

"I never did, not really, luv. Now that I know you better, I can honestly say that I don't believe there is one dishonest bone in your body."

"That's a relief at least."

"Now, no more talk of doom and gloom." He looked up. "Ah, about time you arrived," Alex greeted Mark and Blake.

Blake glanced at his watch. "You did say seven-thirty, mate. And as usual, we're right in time." He looked around the already buzzing restaurant. "Where is that delightful friend of yours, Penelope?"

"In the kitchen, Blake. I'm sure she'll join us as soon as her sous chefs have everything under control. She's a bit of a control freak in that regard."

Amber arrived on cue like she'd been summoned.

"I've arranged for a special tasting menu for our table. I hope you don't mind?" She asked as she slipped into the booth next to Blake.

"I'm sure it will be delicious, just like you," Blake said with a wink.

Amber shot him a disgusted look. "Let's just settle this once and for all, Mr. Hunter. I'm not some twittering twenty-year-old who will melt into a puddle at your corny flirtation." She pointed around the table and eyed him boldly. "So, do us all a favor and desist immediately."

"Ah, you wound me, darling," he chuckled. With renewed respect, his gaze travelled with unerring thoroughness over her face. "Are you sure, sugar? You need to be warned, if I stop flirting, I'll go straight into hot seduction and that my sweet, you'll have no defense against."

"Is this guy for real? Lord, save us all from your vanity," Amber mocked. She turned away and looked across the table at Alex and Penny. "Is there a special reason why we've all been invited to this dinner?"

"Yes, but that can wait until later," Alex's appraising gaze devoured Penny's naked shoulders Their satiny luxuriousness above the strapless dark green dress, which hugged her rounded breasts like a lover's caress, tested his resolve. He felt the familiar twitch in his loins as visions of the past two nights, with her in his arms, flashed like a movie reel through his mind.

She blinked at him; a warm glow painted her cheeks an enticing rosy color as she basked in his appreciation of her appearance. She had chosen her outfit with care. The emerald-green velvet made her eyes appear smoky and warm. The corseted, sweetheart neckline plunged between her breasts, pushing them up invitingly and left her shoulders bare. The fitted skirt was ruched delicately along the side, leading to a slit that left most of her shapely thigh bare. She'd finished the ensemble with a pair of signature Valentino 'Rockstud' pumps that were equal parts elegant and edgy. Made from metallic gold leather, they sported the contrasting, studded blush leather trim.

She felt beautiful, especially when she noticed how Alex's eyes blazed every time he looked at her.

The evening flowed into pleasant, fun-filled hours where they traded tales of their youth. Their laughter was heard often and drew everyone's gaze in their direction. Alex, Blake and Mark were well-known in the tabloids as the Rogues of Manhattan. Their presence, in the company of two lovely women, caused quite a bit of stir.

After the main course, the maître d' served them each a glass of French champagne. Alex took Penny's hand in his. The smile he offered her was full of warmth.

"You're all aware of the circumstances under which Penny and I met. Not to mention the negative impact of Drew's embezzlement and death." Alex shrugged as he looked around the table. "For that reason," Alex kissed Penny's lips briefly—a soft brush of lips that made her crave more, "*and* I'm hoping because she likes me a little, Penny has agreed to marry me."

"Congratulations, mate," Blake beamed. "Not that any of us had any doubt that she would . . . say yes, I mean. You do have the Midas touch, as they say, when it comes to the ladies. Ouch! Damn, sugar, what was that for?" He rubbed his side where

Amber had poked him quite brutality, in his opinion, and offered her a wounded stare.

"For being an inconsiderate lout, you ass!" Amber snapped. She gestured to Penny. "By implication, you're saying that Penny is gullible and incapable of using her brain and only agreed to marry Alex because of his sexual persuasiveness."

"Who said anything about sex, my sweet? Or is it something that's on your mind?" He wiggled his eyebrows. "Do I play a part in your visions at all?"

"Whatever the reason, I'm happy she said yes. So, with our best friends as witness . . ." Alex took out a black velvet ring box from his pocket and opened it. He lifted Penny's hand and slid the ring on her finger, his penetrating gaze searching hers intently.

Penny was so ensnared by his blue gaze that had the power to see into her soul, she barely glanced at the ring until Amber gasped in awe. Her eyes lowered. Her breathing faltered.

"Oh my," she breathed through quivering lips. It was a Scarselli; a dark green marquise-cut diamond ring, set off by a halo of pavé round diamonds in a double band.

"The diamond is the exact color of your green eyes, which is why I chose it."

Penny palmed his face and gave him the sweetest kiss he'd ever received. Her eyes sparkled more than glimmering stones on her finger.

"Thank you, Alex. I didn't expect something this expensive or . . . *real*. It's gorgeous. Perfect, actually."

"You're to be my wife. You deserve it," he breathed against her ear, a shiver traveled down her body.

The decision that Penny had made two days ago, became a reality. She'd not expected him to be this sentimental. That he treated her with such open appreciation and affection, stumped her. He was so different from the impassive man she'd met less than two weeks ago. She was beginning to appreciate the person that he really was. It reflected in his eyes, it was where he carried his humanity. She saw it every time he looked at his friends, the love and respect he had for them. It was humbling to know she was now part of that.

And then there was the way he made love to her; she shivered as she remembered the heat of his touch on her skin. It was always there, even when she stood under the spray of water in the shower—feeling his hands gliding down her body with the water falling over her skin.

I love this man.

146

Penny started at the unexpected thought. *Good lord, woman, get a grip! Don't confuse physical attraction with that! You don't know the man—not really. You can't be in love with him. No fucking way!*

Alex got up and held out his hand to her. "Come, luv, dance with me."

Penny looked around at the people watching them with pleased smiles.

"There's no dance floor, Alex. We can't—"

"Of course, we can. All you need to do is sway in my arms, luv, while I make music with my beautiful fiancée. Perfect way to celebrate this moment."

His smile drew her in and without conscious thought, she found herself swaying gently in his arms to the soft jazz playing in the background. The fellow diners broke out in applause that caused another blush to bloom over her cheeks. She buried her face in his throat to breathe in his woodsy essence. He was all man.

"Thank you."

Penny leaned back and stared into his eyes.

"For what?"

"For being who you are. For offering me a gateway to a life I never thought I'd ever have. With you, life suddenly seems full of endless possibilities." He banned the thought of it being temporary to the back of his mind. At this moment, it felt too real.

"You're making me blush," Penny smiled sweetly. She brushed her fingertips over his chiseled jaw line.

"Hmm, was it my words, or this?" Alex grinned with wicked intent as he dragged her flush against his body. His tumescence dug hard into the softness of her stomach.

"Oh!" Penny's eyes widened at his blatant seduction.

Alex's mind swirled as he sensed the answering desire in her. Her cheeks were red but she didn't look away.

A dare flashed in her forest green eyes.

A tingling sensation disrupted his ruse as she effectively turned the tables on him. He was the one caught in her web now. He had never enjoyed the game of seduction as much as he did with her. It was intoxicating as he gave himself over to the unexplained emotions that ruled his mind in that moment.

"Yes, my beautiful fiancée, tonight there'll be no sleep for you. Not with the sensual promises your eyes have been making."

During the course of the night, filled with euphoric delight and overindulgence, Penny could no longer deny the truth that had shaken her to the core earlier that night.

She was in love with Alexander Sinclair.

"Zhang Wei Chén, please allow me to introduce you to my fiancée, Penelope Winters."

Alex made the introduction as they arrived at the table where Zhang and his wife were already waiting. The restaurant that Blake had chosen was one of Alex's favorites, Per Se, in Manhattan.

Penelope watched Zhang blink, the surprise evident in his gaze at Alex's introduction. He was a distinguished looking silver-haired man, slim, of medium height and in his mid-fifties. He stood up to take Penny's hand and gazed animatedly at the glittering ring on her finger. Her gaze followed his. Her heart skipped a beat. Every time she looked at it, she was awed.

Zhang dropped her hand, pressed his palms together in front of his chest and nodded respectfully.

"It's a pleasure to meet you, Ms. Winters." He pointed behind him to a beautiful woman in her early-fifties. "Please meet my wife, Meili."

Penny and Alex mimicked Zhang's gesture in respectful acknowledgement of her status. Zhang gestured at Penny. "This is a surprise, Alexander. Drew gave us an impression that you had no interest in having a family."

Alex held the chair for Penny; she sank into it with a smile. Her gasp was audible when Alex planted a tender kiss on the nape of her neck. She was wearing her favorite LBD and had done up her hair in a sophisticated, high chignon that left her neck bare. A tantalizing invitation that he couldn't resist.

"My private life is different from my public persona, Zhang," Alex said as he sat down and placed Penny's hand on his thigh. "I've always endeavored to keep my personal life private; especially at work." He traced the ring on Penny's finger. "But this little darling is special."

Zhang stared at them with a pleased smile playing on his lips. "Does that mean you're getting married anytime soon?"

"In two weeks," Alex drawled, with his gaze on Penny. Her eyes flew to his but she did her best to hide her shocked surprise. But she bit her tongue. It wouldn't help; negating Alex's claim in front of Zhang.

But two weeks? Holy shit!

"And we would be honored if you and Meili could be a part of our joyous union," Alex invited them cordially.

"It would indeed be our pleasure," Zhang beamed delightfully. Meili nodded in agreement.

"My apologies for our tardiness," Blake said, arriving next to their table with Amber on his arm. She appeared a little flustered but very beautiful in a dark blue cocktail dress.

"Mr. Harper, it's good to see you again," Zhang gushed. It was evident that he was elated with the change of events.

If Blake was surprised at Zhang's friendliness, it was well hidden behind his usual impassive mask.

"And who is this delightful lady?" Zhang asked as he looked at Amber.

A broad smile spread over Blake's face. He hugged Amber against his side. "This beautiful angel is my 'future' fiancée." Blake winked at Zhang and said in a loud whisper, "I just need to convince her that I'm the only one for her. She's a tad hardheaded."

"You do know that I can hear you, Blake Harper?" Amber scoffed. She turned a beatific smile on Zhang, who blinked in the wake thereof. "Mr. Zhang, I've heard so much about you."

It hadn't taken much convincing from Penny for her to agree to be Blake's date for the evening. Based on Zhang's animated expression, it had been the perfect move, especially since Blake was playing the enamored playboy to perfection.

Somebody give him an Oscar already.

Alex was subtler but his loving gaze and tender touch didn't go unnoticed.

After the first course, Penny and Amber excused themselves to go to the restroom.

"Wow, look at this place," Penny said in awe as they crossed the foyer that led to the restroom which was just as sumptuous. It looked like a luxurious spa, filled with plush sofas and comfortable ottomans. Penny sat down. Her hands flailed in the air.

"Alex told Zhang that we're getting married in two weeks."

"I know."

Penny gaped at Amber. "How the devil do *you* know when it's the first word *I've* heard of it?"

"Because on the night you got engaged, he mentioned it after I offered to host the reception at my restaurant. Alex did say he wanted the wedding to be small and intimate."

"Thanks for giving me a heads up! I need a custom wedding dress and it will never be ready in two weeks."

152

"Calm down, Penny. You've got an entire team that is more than capable of finishing it in time."

"That's not the point, Amber. *It's my wedding.* It's time Alexander Sinclair realizes I'm no pushover. A wedding date is something a couple should decide together. No, we'll get married when it suits *me* and that's the end of it. You can cancel the booking in two weeks. I'll let you know what date we both agree on."

"Penny—"

"Don't Penny me, Amber. I've said my piece. I'm not getting married in two weeks, *period.* Drew rushed me into a wedding and I'll be damned if I'll allow it to happen again."

"I'm sorry, Penny. I should've remembered how upset you were that you never got to wear the wedding dress of your dreams. You're right. You should have your say in this decision."

"Damn right I should," she mumbled as they made their way back to the others.

Penny straightened her shoulders as they approached the table and she felt Alex's eyes on her. He immediately sensed the tension in her. She proceeded to coolly disregard him for the balance of the evening, although she laughed and chatted with everyone else.

It didn't take a genius to figure out what had upset her. Alex sighed heavily. He shouldn't have sprung the wedding date on her like that. At the very least, he should have discussed it with her beforehand.

The explosion came the moment they arrived home.

"I'm not getting married in two weeks," Penny asserted acerbically.

Alex had to hold back his smile. With her hands on her slanted hips, Penny was tapping her foot. His cock twitched in a pleasant reaction to the vision she portrayed. The black dress fit her like a second skin. It was tailored to faithfully follow her curves, with a slim skirt that sculpted her rounded buttocks, and off the shoulder cap sleeves. She looked like an angry vixen.

"Penny, we decided to go ahead with the wedding, so why wait?"

"Exactly, Alex! *We* decided, as in you and me. That implies that there are *two* parties in this relationship." She pointed between them. "Therefore, I should be party to the decision of our wedding date.

"You're right, luv. I should've discussed it with you."

"Yes, you should have. I'm glad we're in agreement. We can discuss it in the morning and decide on a date together."

"I don't see the need, Penelope, seeing as you now know—"

"There is *every* need. For one thing, my wedding dress won't be ready in two weeks."

"Already arranged. You have nothing to worry about. I've got everything under control."

Penny's gaze turned glacial.

"You *arranged* a wedding dress?"

"Sure. I've got a pretty good idea of your likes and dislikes. Also, I've got excellent taste."

"*Of course,* you do."

The chilled condescension in her voice left Alex with no doubt that she was being sarcastic.

Penny turned toward the stairs. "As I said, we'll discuss it tomorrow and *no*." She flung him a cutting glare when he opened his mouth to protest. "I am *not* wearing a wedding dress designed by someone else. Nor am I going to be rushed through the planning process."

She pivoted around to face him and anchored him in place with a debilitating look. "I will not be rushed like I was the first time. *Period*."

Alex stared after her as she stomped upstairs. Admiration shone in his eyes. His future wife had a lot more spunk than he gave her credit for.

His future suddenly seemed a lot brighter and exceedingly exciting.

"I can't wait to call you my wife. My own little spitfire."

CHAPTER TEN

"I have to apologize once again for the inconvenience, Ms. Winters." Gabrielle said smoothly.

She didn't just sit down, Penny observed, she slid gracefully into the office chair behind her desk. She was a beautiful, statuesque woman.

Between the excitement of the engagement and meeting Zhang Wei Chén, the request to sign documents had completely slipped Penny's mind; as did discussing it with Alex. She'd been on her way to the factory when Gabrielle had phoned her again. She'd been annoyed at first but then decided to get it over with. Especially, since Alex hadn't brought anything home with him for her to sign.

"It's not a problem."

"I've ordered some coffee and tea, as I didn't know your preference," Gabrielle said with a tight smile.

"That's not necessary. I'm actually running behind, Ms. Brittle. I was on my way to work when you phoned. I have a meeting in thirty minutes."

"Of course, but I would feel dreadful if you didn't at least have a few sips." She leaned back in the chair and stared intently at Penny, like she was willing her to accede something to her.

"Can we just get to the paperwork, Ms. Brittle?" Penny prodded when she seemed rather unhurried about getting the documents.

Gabrielle's mouth pulled into a tight smile. "Of course," she chipped in a cold voice. She pivoted in her chair and got up to retrieve a blue folder from the credenza on one side of the large office.

Penny found her behavior strange. She seemed fidgety as she paged through the file, her lips in a flat line and her face marred by a deep frown. She glanced at Penny and offered an engaging smile.

"You said you changed your surname?"

"Yes, back to my maiden name."

"Was it a long process? I know some of my clients have complained about the long waiting periods."

"Not too long."

"If I may ask, what prodded you to take such a drastic step?" Gabrielle continued. She withdrew a document from the file and pretended to read through it.

"It's a long story and not something I like to talk about."

"I'm sorry. I didn't mean to bring up unpleasant memories." She looked up when her assistant arrived with a tray filled with refreshments.

"Ah, wonderful. Thank you, Anne. Would you mind pouring for us, please?" She looked at Penny expectantly. "Coffee or tea, Ms. Winters?"

Penny dragged in a calming breath. It was evident that the attorney had no compunction about dragging this out. "Tea, thank you. One milk, no sugar."

"You're better than me. I've got a terrible sweet tooth." Gabrielle's hands fluttered in the air. "I can't get coffee or tea past my lips without at least two heaped spoons of sugar."

Penny accepted the delicate porcelain cup from Anne and tentatively took a small sip. It was searing hot. She placed the cup on the desk in front of her.

"Shall we get on with it, please?"

"Did you bring proof of identity with you as I requested, Ms. Winters? Unfortunately, it's a requirement that needs to be verified. I need your passport and either your driver's license or social security card."

Penny curbed her rising irritation. Some sixth sense was warning her that something was amiss.

She dug out her passport and driver's license and pushed it toward her. Luckily, she'd been carrying her passport for something at work.

"This will only take a moment. I need to make a copy of it and then verify your driver's license on the DMV system."

Penny nodded. With a long, dragged out sigh, she picked up the cup and saucer to take another sip. She glanced at her watch, her foot bounced as a sign of her impatience.

"There you go." Gabrielle's sanguine voice came from the door as she returned and handed back Penny's documents. "How's the tea? Not too strong?"

"It's perfect, thank you. Ms. Brittle, I must insist that we rush this along. I'm going to be late for my meeting as it is," Penny asserted.

"I'm terribly sorry. It wasn't my intention to inconvenience you but Mr. Sinclair is a stickler for procedures, especially legal ones."

"I understand. It's your job. Where do I need to sign," Penny prodded when Gabrielle just smiled at her.

She nodded with a wide smile. "It's not a very lengthy document and a little different than the norm. In such cases, the policy proceeds are offered as security for the balance of a debt, not transferred in full to another party."

"I'm aware of that," Penny interjected.

"However, you have indicated that you wish to cede the full value of the policy to the Allied Group. Is that correct?"

"Yes, that's correct."

"Ms. Winters, I have to ask. Are you aware of the value of the proceeds of this policy? It's a lot of money to say no to," Gabrielle asked with a questioning look in her eyes.

"To be honest, Ms. Brittle, I have no idea how much it is and quite frankly, I don't care. I want nothing to do with anything that is associated with Drew Carver."

She took the proffered document and pen from Gabrielle.

"Stop," Gabrielle said as Penny immediately began to initial the pages without glancing at the contents. "I'm afraid I have to insist that you read through the cession agreement. It is due diligence."

Penny pressed her lips together but rather than embarking on a debate with the pushy attorney, she quickly scanned the contents.

"It's all in order," she said shortly and made quick work of signing where indicated. She placed the pen on top of the document and got up.

"Thank you for the tea. I'm afraid I have to go. Unless there is anything else you need from me?"

Gabrielle smiled sweetly. She followed Penny to the door. "No, that's everything. Once again, thank you for taking the time to come here."

Penny didn't respond but Gabrielle didn't expect her to. She watched her walk away, feeling a sense of satisfaction fill her entire being. She tried to keep the grin of victory off her lips as she noticed Anne watching her curiously.

"I need to make a private phone call. See that I'm not disturbed for the next hour," she snapped and returned to her office. The door closed with a decisive click behind her and she quickly dialed Clive Ratcliff. Clive and she had been a team since school. Their on and off relationship had survived after all the years, which was a miracle at best, since Clive was an exceedingly jealous man.

"I've got it," she clipped when he answered. "When can you come around to collect it?"

"What exactly have you got? Why can't you just bring it home with you?"

"Because I want you to get started on it immediately. I've got her fingerprints on the cup and saucer, as well as the pen. Did Richard agree to help us?"

"Yes. He has the tech to produce the replica fingerprints for you to glue onto yours."

"I assume he has done this before?"

A heavy sigh sounded in her ears. "Of course, babe, otherwise I wouldn't have asked him. Don't worry, if the prints are clear, he'll get it done."

"Good. I'm waiting for you. Make it quick, I have some business errands to run." She ended the call. After putting on some gloves, she carefully placed the cup and saucer that Penny had used inside the credenza and closed it. A self-satisfied smile flashed on her face.

She scrutinized the document Penny had signed, tracing her signature with a pointed nail tip.

"This was almost too easy. Such a simple signature. It'll be a piece of cake." She picked up her pen and started to practice copying it.

"Perfect!" She preened a short while later. She compared her efforts with Penny's. It was almost identical. "No one would detect the difference. Not at first glance, at any rate."

She reached for her cell phone when it began to buzz. "Shit," she exclaimed as she recognized the name on the small screen. She cleared her throat before she swiped to answer.

"Dave, what a pleasant surprise," she greeted the HR head of the Allied Group, her voice dripping with the sweetness of honey.

"Morning, Gabrielle."

She immediately detected a sharp edge in his voice.

"What can I do for you today?"

"I just had a conversation with Drew Carver's beneficiary. I'd like to know the purpose of your involvement in this."

"I'm sorry, Dave, I should've discussed it with you but I felt it was important to finalize all the legal documentation in regard to the cession agreement as soon as possible."

"I don't understand the need, Gabrielle. What legal documentation? The insurance company has their own legal department. They personally deal with this kind of thing."

"I'm aware of that, Dave, but as the inside counsel, it's my duty to take additional precaution. This way, it's airtight and we wouldn't—"

"Does Alex know about this?"

"I don't see the need to discuss such menial issues with him. I was just doing what I'm getting paid for," she hedged acerbically.

"See to it that the agreement is delivered to my office, Gabrielle."

"Of course."

"Today, Gabrielle."

She started to respond but he abruptly ended the connection.

"Fucking prick!" She sneered. "I better phone Alex and plead my case before Dave fucks up everything."

Clive arrived without knocking. She shot him a cold glare.

"This is my workplace, Clive. I expect you to knock before you just barge in. What if I had been with a client?"

"But you're not, so stop whining," he returned, just as irritated. He was tired of being treated as her side-kick. It was time Gabrielle gave him the respect and love he deserved.

"Where is it?" He opened the container he'd brought with him.

Gabrielle removed the cup and saucer from the credenza carefully. He took it from her with equal care, placed each piece in a plastic bag before he placed them inside the container. He did the same with the pen but scrutinized it first. It was a silver ballpoint pen.

"I wiped it clean before she arrived and made sure I didn't touch it afterward. The thumb print on the pen should be very clear." Gabrielle peered over his shoulder.

"This part of our plan has to go without any glitches, Clive. I'm depending on you to ensure that. We need to move quickly to get that money. I don't trust Penelope Winters. No woman would say no to millions of dollars like she just did."

"Except if she knew there was ten times more waiting for her," Clive asserted.

"Exactly."

"What about the code? That's one obstacle we still haven't found a solution for."

"I know enough about legal requirements to get around it, darling. The fingerprint and proof of identity will do the trick." Gabrielle handed him a folder. "Make sure the fake passport and driver's license is perfect. I don't want to end up in jail."

"That's the easy part." Clive leaned in to kiss Gabrielle on the lips. "The quicker we get this done, the better. I'm fed up of hiding in that musty old motel. It's time to get the fuck away from here."

"Patience, my darling. Our time is near. A week or two is a small concession to make."

She picked up her handbag and the blue folder from her desk and headed toward the door. "For now, I need to appease the mighty Alexander Sinclair, before Dave Clinton fucks things up."

A little while later, she walked into Alex's office with her usual confidence and grace. She was cautious at first but eased up when he smiled. Clearly, Clive hadn't ratted her out yet.

"Did we have an appointment, Gabrielle?" Alex asked once she was seated.

"No, but I had to drop off some documents for Dave, so I thought to pop in and say hello."

"It's always a pleasure to see you. Unfortunately, I don't have much time."

"Of course, I just took the chance to inform you that I've had Drew Carver's beneficiary sign the papers, ceding the policy proceeds to the company." She tapped the folder on her lap. "The reason for my presence."

The change in Alex was dramatic. Gabrielle was shaken by the black look he shot at her.

"What the hell for? Did Dave request it?"

Alex was furious. He'd just managed to win Penelope's trust. An action like this could easily set them back two steps.

"No, but it's my job to safeguard the company against any litigation, Alex. You should know that better than anyone," she hedged hurriedly.

"Penelope Winters isn't a threat to us, Gabrielle."

"I beg to differ, Alex. You forget, the money Drew embezzled is still out there and she—"

"I repeat. My *fiancée* has nothing to do with that," Alex clipped her short.

Gabrielle's mouth fell open. The cogs in her brain scrambled to connect the dots based on what he'd just revealed. It changed *everything*. For one thing, it meant that Penny was under his protection. The most infuriating realization was that her carefully laid plans to marry the most sought-after billionaire in New York had just flown out the window. A slow anger unfurled inside her, rapidly escalating to a chilled fury that threatened to explode to the surface.

She forced a deep breath into her lungs in an effort to bring her raging emotions under control.

"I apologize, Alex. Had I known—"

"In future, be sure to double-check with Dave. You have carte blanche on certain legal matters as far as the business is concerned, Gabrielle, but internal HR protocols don't fall under your purview."

"Of course. I assure you it won't happen again."

She fiddled with her bag before peering at him through her eyelashes.

"It must be a relief."

A raised eyebrow was his only response.

"I mean, with her as your fiancée, at least it means that you'll be able to recover the money Drew embezzled."

"We're very close, yes. It should be wrapped up within a couple of weeks."

Gabrielle couldn't get out of the building fast enough. She'd just stepped outside when she barked into her cell phone, "Things have changed. We need to move our plans forward."

She waved down a cab and got inside. A frown marred her smooth forehead.

"For that matter, we need to regroup. We might have to tackle this issue differently. Playing nice is no longer an option."

CHAPTER ELEVEN

"Yoo-hoo! Where's the happy bride?" Amber's lilting voice traveled across the room as she stepped through the door.

"I'm glad you and Alex could agree on the wedding date." Amber glanced sideways at Penny who had just walked out of the bathroom. "Are you sure about this, Penny? I expected the wedding to be moved back by months, not just a week."

Penny's smile was melancholy. "It was the only concession Alex was prepared to make but it gave me enough time to have made the wedding dress I wanted." She looked at the gorgeous lace, chiffon and tulle wedding dress hanging against the closet. "And yes, Amber. I'm sure about this. I know it's hard to believe but I . . ." she hesitated. Her hands fluttered in the air. "I fell in love with him."

"Does he know?"

"Oh, hell no! I'm still trying to come to terms with it myself and besides, love is not a prerequisite for him to get married."

"And yet for you, it is. That's a surefire recipe for disaster, Penny, not to mention the risk of breaking your heart."

"You're not telling me anything I haven't regurgitated over and over, Amber. If there's one thing that Gran taught me, it's to fight for what I believe in. I don't know why but I *believe* in Alex, in a future with him. Come hell or high water, I'm not giving up without a fight to make it work."

"Come now, Penny. That'll be a piece of cake for you."

Penny laughed quietly as she slipped into a pair of white lace panties, sinfully sexy garters and silky stockings, before she sat down in front of the mirror.

Amber began by applying the base make-up to her face.

"Pray tell. I can't wait to hear what this miracle potion is that you've got in mind."

"No potion, my dear friend. Love. All you need to do is make him fall in love with you too."

"Oh, of course," she quipped with a smile. "Why didn't I think of that?"

"I'm serious, Penny. I've seen the way Alex looks at you."

"That's lust, girl. There's no denying that as far as sex is concerned we totally combust between the sheets. Alex desires me and that's—"

"Pfft," Amber cut her short. "It's more than that. There's something in his eyes that I haven't been able to decipher but it's not just lust, of that I'm sure of."

Penny contemplated what Amber had just said. She too had been aware of the enigmatic looks from Alex.

"If I have to be honest, I've had the feeling that his attitude toward me has changed, especially when we make love. He's more tender and, in my mind, even loving."

"There, *see*! Now build on that. Love needs nurturing. I believe in you, Penny. All you have to do is be yourself to make him love you."

Penny went silent as she mused over Amber's comments. Drew's deceit had left scars deeper than she'd initially believed. She'd thought she had managed to bury those insecurities and was beginning to regain her self-confidence.

She moaned as Amber gently massaged her skull before she started gathering the long tresses into an elegant French knot behind her head and anointed it with diamond flower pins.

"Hmm, that feels so good," Penny sighed. "I'm glad you convinced me to go to the spa with you yesterday. It was just what I needed to relax."

"Just because you're getting married under unusual circumstances doesn't mean you shouldn't be pampered like any other bride." She hugged her briefly. "You missed out on it once and I'd be damned if I allow it to happen again."

"I don't know how I would've survived without you since Gran passed away, Amber. No one could ask for a better friend than you."

"Sisters, girl. We surpassed friendship when we ditched our diapers."

Penny laughed. "That we have and a couple of other things over the years!"

Amber stood back and examined her handiwork with a critical eye. Penny's makeup was impeccable, giving her a naturally, dewy look which elevated her features to another level of mystique. With a touch of smokiness to her eyes, her coral lips and iridescent skin, she had never looked better.

"Perfect. You're going to take his breath away. Oh no," she shrieked and turned Penny away from the mirror. "No peeking until you have your wedding dress on."

She carefully assisted Penny to get the dress on and gaped at her in admiration.

"Oh my god. You look absolutely *gorgeous!*"

Penny turned to stare at her reflection in the full-length mirror. It was like her sketch come to life. She blinked furiously as she felt the unexpected burn of tears behind her eyelids.

The dress fitted Penny to perfection. She looked exactly like she'd envisioned she would—only better. She hardly recognized herself. Suddenly, she felt a surge of excitement about the wedding. For the first time, it felt real.

God, how I wish it was, and that he loved me too.

"It's time." Amber's voice broke her reverie. She straightened her shoulder determinedly. Amber was right. There was something between her and Alex. Now that her own feelings were clear, Penny came to a decision.

Alexander Sinclair will *love me. Come hell or high water.*

"Morris at the Harley Davidson store on Staten Island said he'll give you a special discount, seeing as you're ordering two Heritage Softail bikes."

"Dream on, mate," Alex scoffed at Mark with a broad smile. He tightened the knot of the silver tie around his neck. He smirked at his two friends as he shrugged into his tailored, black tuxedo jacket. "In case Morris asks, I want the white and chrome one he advertised last month." He smoothed his jacket in place. "You can place the order in the meantime."

Blake prodded Mark in the side. "The groom doth protest too much, don't you think?"

Mark chuckled as he looked Alex up and down. "Very debonair, mate," Mark quipped. "Doesn't he look dashing, Blake?"

"If I didn't know better, I'd swear the two of you were jealous," Alex drawled.

"Of your ugly ass? Never!" Blake said with a wide grin.

"Of me getting married, you ass," Alex taunted them.

"You have to admit, mate. Of the three of us, you are the last one any of us thought would get hitched first."

"Yeah, what he said," Mark cheered.

Alex didn't seem fazed. "You know why I'm getting married and it's temporary."

Mark snorted, "If you say so, buddy." He glanced at his watch. "Time to go."

Blake wasn't fooled by Alex's cheerful mood and searched his expression. "Are you sure you're ready for this?"

Alex ambled toward the door. "Have I ever done anything I wasn't prepared for?"

"Can't say I recall anything, no," Blake agreed.

"Then let's go. We can't keep my bride waiting because of your sudden desire to turn shrink on me."

Alex and Blake arrived at the chapel just in time to take their places in front of the pew. Mark strolled to the back. Keeping an eye on everyone was second nature to him.

The chapel bell chimed melodiously, followed by the arched doors opening as the rich sounds of the organ, playing the *wedding march*, filled the small church.

Alex turned to watch Amber walk down the aisle, dressed in a soft peach, off-shoulder dress that hugged her body like a lover's caress.

"Damn, she looks hot," Blake growled next to Alex.

"Behave yourself, mate. Stop drooling over the maid of honor."

Penny appeared in the doorway next. Alex promptly forgot to breathe.

He had always heard that there was nothing more beautiful than a woman on her wedding day. Penny just confirmed that belief. The tulle material of the skirt flowed around her as she walked. His eyes trailed over the tight lace bodice that hugged her breasts lovingly. He could see the long train that trailed behind her. He was glad that she'd skipped the veil and elected to show off the long, intricate diamond earrings he'd given her as a wedding present.

She looked like an angel, dropped down from the heavens. A small smile played on her lips but he could detected her nervousness as she walked closer. A bouquet of white lilies was a perfect addition to her beauty.

Alex had prepared himself for the impact of her beauty but he hadn't bargained on the myriad of emotions that flooded his mind as she approached. The sudden rush of possessiveness confounded him. He'd never been the jealous type—one for monotony, even less. But as he watched her walk toward him, it was the only thought running through his mind.

Mine. She's mine.

Penny couldn't tear her eyes from his. She was overwhelmed by the look on his face. Gone was the impassive and inscrutable expression he usually sported. She blinked as he made no effort to hide his candor. It left her breathless.

She halted. A small step separated them. Alex didn't move; just continued to stare at her.

"Do you have *any* idea how beautiful you are, Penelope?" He murmured quietly to her.

A becoming blush bloomed over her cheeks at the compliment.

"I'm glad I agreed to move the wedding back. It was worth the wait and I'm a very lucky man. You take my breath away, luv."

"And I'm a very lucky woman. You look very handsome, Alex."

Alex breached the space between them to cup her cheeks in his palms. He captured her misty gaze with an impenetrable stare. Their breath meshed as they shared an intimate exhale before he closed the final inch between them.

He kissed her like he had never kissed her before. Deep, with passionate strokes of his tongue that lay claim to her body and mind. Penny melted into his ripped body, clinging to his back as she returned the kiss with all the love and passion in her body.

"Ahem . . . it seems Mr. Sinclair is skipping to the end of the ceremony," the amused voice of the Minister broke them apart.

Alex brushed his finger over her glowing cheeks. The smile they shared was one of tenderness and mutual affection. He turned and drew her hand through the hook of his arm, keeping it clasped in his as they faced the minister.

Penny found it difficult to concentrate on the Minister's words that droned in the background. She was too shaken by how *right* it felt to stand beside Alex, vowing to love each other until death do them part.

"I now pronounce you husband and wife. You may kiss the bride, Mr. Sinclair . . . again."

Amidst the chuckles of the guests that consisted only of close friends and a couple of Alex's cousins, uncles and aunts, Alex pulled her into his embrace and kissed her deeply, effectively sealing their vows.

After the wedding register had been signed, Amber insisted on the full enchilada of wedding photos.

"It's part of my wedding gift to you. Raoul is one of the best photographers in New York. I trust him to capture this joyous occasion beautifully."

"Amber—"

"She's right," Alex cut Penny short; she had noticed the pained expression on his face and was about to refuse.

"But Alex, you—"

"No buts," he silenced her with a finger on her lips. "You didn't have this the first time around, so this time, everything needs to be perfect. Come now, luv, wipe that frown off your face. I'll survive. I'm a pro at smiling for cameras, no matter how much I hate it."

An hour later, Penny had had enough. She stamped her foot when Raoul insisted on another pose in front of a weeping willow tree.

"Enough Raoul. No more. My feet are killing me. Besides, we're keeping our guests waiting and I, for one, am starving."

"Just a couple more, Mrs. Sinclair," Raoul cajoled her.

"You'll have to excuse us, Raoul. We must listen to the bride. I hope you'll be joining us for the reception." Having said that, Alex picked up Penny in his arms.

"Alex! What are you doing?" She shrieked as she clutched her arms around his neck, unaware of Raoul happily snapping away with his camera.

"Giving your battered feet a break, my sweet," he said as he carried her toward Blake's black Jaguar. He'd generously offered to drive them to Amber's Cuisine.

"At your service, sir," Blake said with a teasing bow as he opened the back door.

"Yeah, right. Just remember, this isn't a race to get to the restaurant, mate," Alex warned. "Take it slow and easy. I'm living a dream right now. Don't jar me awake."

Blake just laughed and held open the front door for Amber, who shot him a heated glance when he placed a hot kiss on the nape of her neck as she walked past him.

"Keep your lips to yourself, Mr. Casanova," she warned as she folded her long legs into the front of the car.

"You wound me, darling," he said with his hand over his heart and closed the door.

Penny loved the banter between the two men all the way to Amber's restaurant. The mutual love and respect was quite discernible. It was uncanny how similar their history was to her and Amber's.

"Oh, my lord, *Amber!* This is out of this world," Penny exclaimed as they walked into the restaurant amidst the applause of their guests. Her face glowed with happiness as she looked around. Amber had turned the restaurant into a whimsical wonderland with gossamer gold drapes flowing from the magical chandelier that graced the center of the room. All around the cavernous room, fairytale lights and stunning flower arrangements comprising of lilies, hydrangeas and peonies added visual interest and took the ambience of the room to another level. The intimately set tables were beautifully dressed too. Amber had even converted her private patio dining space into a dance floor.

"I'm glad you like it. Go on, sit down. Our table is near the dance floor."

Mark and Blake were already seated at the table and welcomed them, with a fair bit of ribbing coming Alex's way. Amber pointed to a table. "Be right back, I just need to check in with the kitchen."

The night was magical. Penny basked in the loving attention Alex showered onto her. She reveled in his arms as they took to the dance floor with a slow waltz. Before long, their guests joined them on the floor and the gaiety went a notch higher.

The night was a memory that Penny would always treasure. Alex had been the perfect groom throughout the entire reception. He'd gone out of his way to put her at ease and make her feel special. Not once did she feel that they weren't celebrating their joyous union for real.

All in all, it was the perfect wedding day.

Warm arms wrapped around her body to pull her against a hard chest. Penny felt a thrill of pleasure carouse down her spine as Alex gently nibbled on her ear. His breath felt scorching hot against her shin.

"Time for us to leave, my sweet."

Penny leaned back against him. Every time he touched her, something wild came to life inside her. Over the past couple of weeks, it had broached the perimeter of her desire and slowly chipped away the wall around her heart.

"I'll just say goodbye to—"

"No goodbyes. We're just going to slip away quietly; otherwise we'll be spending another hour here. I need my wife. *Now.*"

Penny's tingling laughter flowed through Alex, leaving him defenseless against the emotions he never thought he'd experience. Becoming sentimental wasn't in his DNA, nor was falling in love. Now, the *lust* he felt for his lovely luscious wife was a completely different story. That he could cope with.

Ever since the Minister had declared them man and wife, his desire for her had been growing with every passing minute, to the point that his pants were feeling uncomfortably tight.

It was high time they consummated their marriage. Come morning, Penelope Winters would feel well and truly wedded.

And bedded.

Chapter Twelve

"Alex, put me down," Penny protested when he picked her up and carried her over the threshold of his penthouse in Manhattan that he sometimes used to sleep over. He'd decided it would be perfect for their wedding night. "You don't have to do this."

"Of course, I do, luv. Every bride deserves this tradition." He silenced her protest with a brief kiss as he gently lowered her feet to the floor in the master bedroom. "Besides, I kinda like to hold you in my arms like this."

"Oh my, how romantic," she gasped in awe as she looked at the sensual ambience created by the glow of the candles flickering all around the room. Red rose petals were strewn on the bed and the floor. Penny's eyes went straight to the ceiling-high glass doors that were standing open, leading to the balcony. Penny's eyes widened at the picture-perfect view the place afforded. There was a canopied day-bed, comfy chairs, outdoor bar, and a large Jacuzzi that glimmered in the evening light and dozens of candles.

"Did you do this?"

"Yes. Except the candles. I had someone do it before we arrived."

"I never realized you had such a romantic streak in you."

"There's a lot you don't know about me, my sweet wife."

He nudged her toward the bed and pushed her down. He hunched down on one knee in front of her. His large hands were warm and confident as he pushed her dress over her knees, gently kneading her calves before he took off her shoes.

"Hmm," Penny moaned softly and shivered when Alex placed soft, nibbling kisses along the arch and instep of her foot.

"I'm going to prepare the Jacuzzi for us. Why don't you get undressed? I'll put the champagne on ice."

Penny glanced toward the balcony. The Jacuzzi presented an infinity view of city. It would be surreal. She nibbled on her bottom lip.

"Did you bring my bathing suit, Alex?" she called after him.

He popped his head around the glass door. His grin was wicked and seductive at the same time.

"What for, luv? I'll only have to remove it."

"But what if anyone sees us?"

"This is the penthouse, luv. I have no neighbors and the balcony faces the Hudson River, so it's completely private. I'm the only voyeur you need to worry about."

It didn't really ease Penny's discomfort. Inherently, she was quite shy. Having Alex's eyes on her bare skin has been a revelation since they started sleeping together. He made her feel desirable and beautiful. Every inch of her body.

"Oh, thank you!" She exclaimed when she found a fluffy, white cotton robe in the bathroom. At least she wouldn't have to walk out naked!

She carefully stepped out of her dress and made short work of her lacey lingerie. She refreshed in the sumptuous bathroom and put on the robe.

Her eyes widened as she stepped out onto the balcony. Her apartment had a terrific view too but nothing could beat breath-taking view of the Hudson River set against the backdrop of this magnificent city.

"What a gorgeous view," she exclaimed, her head swiveling from left to right in appreciation.

"Indeed," Alex's deep voice drew her gaze to the Jacuzzi where he was already waiting for her. His eyes gleamed from the underwater illumination of the Jacuzzi. "Such a pity, the best part is buried under that robe."

Penny couldn't keep her eyes from straying over the musculature of his body. She drooled at the sight of his wide chest and washboard torso that disappeared under the water. Her breath puffed from her lips.

"You're naked," she breathed softly.

"And you're overdressed. Take off that robe, my sweet."

Penny glanced around, her shyness returning afresh.

"Now, Penelope."

Her hands lifted of their own accord and slipped the robe from her shoulders. She felt its softness caress her buttocks and thighs as it fell to the floor.

Penny felt his eyes on her naked body. A shiver of embarrassment, mingled with excitement, tingled at her neck. Her nipples became erect under his ravenous stare. His licked his lips, slowly and deliberately, leaving her feeling weak at the knees. She pressed her thighs together but it didn't help to stop her awakening desire.

Alex held out his hand. "Come, luv. Join me."

Penny dragged in a deep, calming breath and carefully stepped into the tub. Before she could catch her breath, he pulled her into his arms and pressed a heated kiss onto her mouth. The air sizzled around them, filled with the passion and unbridled lust that ignited Alex's turgid arousal to press into her softness.

"You are so beautiful," he said and nibbled on the pulpy fullness of her bottom lip. "Sexy," he breathed against her lip. Another sharp nip. "So alluring that I can't resist you."

Penny was aswirl in rising euphoria. Her eyes turned cloudy as she watched him reach for the two glasses of champagne and hand her one.

"A toast," he said with a roguish smile that stalled her breath. It gave him a dangerous appeal and promised untold pleasures. He touched his glass to hers, the resounding 'clink' echoing in the discreet hum of the night. "To *us* and our future." He shook his head when he read the insecurity in her eyes. "No, Penelope, no negative thoughts. Not tonight. In this moment, there is only us, and a depraved mutual hunger that needs feeding."

Penny smiled, suddenly at ease.

"To us," she agreed and took a tentative sip. Her eyes strayed to the view. "This feels absolutely wicked," she sighed as Alex switched on the jets and the lukewarm water started swirling around her naked skin.

"You're about to learn the true meaning of wicked, luv," Alex's murmured into her hair. His hands closed around her waist as he drew her back against his naked chest, fusing his skin with every inch of hers from shoulder to hip.

Penny leaned her head against his shoulder, arching into him as she reveled in the hardness of his arousal, pressed into her back. He lowered his head to nibble on the soft skin at the base of her neck. Her breath caught as his hands teasingly traced the contours of her hips and slowly trailed upward. A whimper escaped from her lips as her nipples turned into hard stones. He brushed his fingertips over them, followed by a grazing of his palms, back and forth over the taut peaks.

"This must be what heaven feels like—your soft naked body, so responsive to my touch."

His words had her quaking with arousal. Her skin suddenly seems to have shrunk over her body. She could feel her core tightening involuntarily with every caress of his hand over her stomach and hips.

"Oh!" Penny gasped in delight when he brushed his fingers over her satiny mound and flicked a finger against her distended clit.

"Do you like that, luv?" Alex breathed into her ear. He was delighted at her uninhibited response to his touch.

"Yes," she hissed, canting her hips.

"Hmm, patience, sweetheart," he coerced, before he bit into the base of her neck.

"Oh god," Penny wailed. She jerked wildly, gasping for a breath at the unexpected sting in her neck, which he soothed with long, smooth licks of his wicked tongue.

"Alex," she whimpered for more as his hand drifted away. Alex relented to her sweet plea by stroking around the hard clitoris but never touching it.

"So responsive," he drawled as he drew a figure eight around it.

"*Please*," the plea fell from her lips with a breathy puff.

Alex didn't respond. Her sensual responses spiked his lust. His cock was swollen and taut as the hot spark of arousal flared in his loins.

Penny shifted in his arms, silently begging, her actions driven by the throbbing in her clitoris that screamed for a release.

"Ready, luv?"

"Go-hd *yes*," she uttered in an incoherent stutter as all her energy suddenly surged between her legs. Her hips jerked as Alex pressed down on the throbbing fleshy button. "More," Penny demanded as his caress turned to slow, smooth strokes, which summoned all the hunger into one spot.

Alex gauged her reaction, waiting for the perfect moment to pull the trigger that would send her tumbling into the abyss of pleasure. He could feel the trembling in her stomach as her body canted against his in complete submission to the erotic dance of seduction.

"Alex, please," she begged as he stroked her nipple with the other hand and then pinched the hardened peak. "Oh, Jesus," she moaned as heat rippled through her core.

"Yes, luv, give it all to me," her murmured into her ear as he inserted a finger knuckle-deep into her hot channel. Her cry coalesced with his growl as her moist heat engulfed his finger. "God, I love how hot you always are."

He smoothed her warm, wet essence all over her throbbing clit, caressing it with long strokes. His fingers closed around her nipple, tugging at it, pulling on it, and pinching it hard. Alex turned her face sideways to watch her eyes as he toggled her clit with short rapid bursts.

"I can't . . . ohhhh!" Hot blood surged through her veins. Her scream echoed into the atmosphere as she shattered in his arms.

"Beautiful, baby," Alex praised. He could feel the nub swell as he continued to draw a sensual pattern over it, thrilled by her twitching body as he kept fueling her climax. He had never seen anything hotter that this woman—his wife—climaxing.

"Alex . . ." Penny slumped in his grasp, gasping to draw a breath as he continued to brush his fingertips in a gentle caress over her glowing skin.

Alex wrapped his arms around her to hold her against his chest, listening to her wheezing breath as she struggled to bring her, still contorting, body under control. He turned her around in his arms to face him and pressed his lower body flush against her. His eyes scorched into hers as his hard arousal throbbed against her soft belly.

"Alex, are you sure no one—"

He chuckled. "You just screamed your head off, luv and now you worry?"

"Oh, sweet lord! Did I do that?" Penny's hands covered her blooming cheeks.

"And I loved it." His smile straightened. He removed her hands and brushed his fingers over her cheeks. "I want you, my sweet, seductive and yet so innocent, wife. Right here, right now. I can honestly say that I've never wanted anyone more than I want you in this moment."

Penny shivered at the depth and sincerity that echoed from his deep voice. Every nerve in her body reacted as it began to smolder with renewed lust. She was amazed to be aroused this soon again but was defenseless as her loins turned into inflamed molten plasma, heating the shell of her core.

She leaned closer and kissed his lips. Her whispered, "Yes, please, my husband," combusted in his mind. His cock became fully engorged and throbbed against her soft belly.

Alex breathed in her sweet elixir and pressed his face in her fragrant hair. "I love your smell. It's delicious, like every inch of your beautiful body. This is one night that I never want to end."

He was surprised at the shudder that shook his frame. He became lost in the thought. He was drowning in the surrealism of the moment. One that would become a crystallized memory.

Damnit Alexander. Keep it together. You know this isn't permanent.

Penny smiled into his eyes and stroked his chin. He felt like a traitor as he saw the warmth and loving capitulation in her eyes.

"I feel it too, Alex."

Rather than allowing his emotions to run free in a moment of weakness, he focused on mentally locking them out. Now wasn't the time to give in to the temptation.

Penny sensed his withdrawal; however subtle he might have been. "Alex—"

His lips covered hers with a lustful kiss that assuaged her anxiety and rekindled the lust in her veins. She banked the concerns to evaluate at a later time.

She'd fallen in love with him, and she knew giving him her heart unconditionally, could end up getting hurt worse than with Drew. Alex had the power to destroy her. This time the love in her heart was different—the all or nothing kind. She wasn't a young, impressionable young woman anymore. Penny could feel her heart race painfully in her chest. Was she ready for this or was she truly walking into disaster with her eyes wide open?

Locked in each other's embrace, they swayed and turned, lost together in the moment. Alex struggled to bring his raging passion under control. It was a futile battle as Penny's demands surpassed his own.

For the first time Alex felt himself waiver under the powerful emotions that threatened to engulf him.

"Alex, please. I need you." Penny was lost in the moment and in him. She pushed him back into the seat of the tub and straddled his hips, pressing down against his cock, grinding her swollen vulva up and down his hard length.

Alex ground his teeth but endeavored to keep his lust in check. He tickled her hips, dipping and swirling on her satiny skin to tease and entice. Penny was unable to process the intensity of the pleasure that followed each caress. Her body felt like it was in ephemeral paralysis, where nothing but his touch and his breath could bring her to life.

"Penelope, you are so much more than I ever expected to find. I'm . . ." Alex checked the words that threatened on his lips.

No. You don't. He quickly negated the wayward thought that tumbled in his mind. It was the one emotion he would never submit to. *Don't even go there, Alex! Not ever.*

Penny started to tremble. She was incapable of moving due to fear that trumped the desire to not only seduce the man but to win the emotions she could sense was so tightly protected inside his heart.

Alex resolutely set out to ban any emotions and thoughts from his mind with sensory enticement and lust. He placed warm kisses on her eyelids and lips, deliberately fueling her desire afresh.

Alex stared at Penny's lust-drugged body leaning taut in his arms. It was a disarming sight; to see her naked in the candle light. He closed his heart against the vulnerability that appeared in her eyes as his gaze travelled over her body. Her breasts were perfectly molded to her form. He couldn't resist brushing a finger across the taut nipples.

"I love these," he murmured as he leaned closer to teethe on the sulky pink of her lip while fondling the taut roundness of the perky orbs.

"Alex, I can't . . . not anymore," Penny whimpered. She boldly reached between their bodies to draw her palm up and down his pulsating shaft, throbbing and warm to her touch.

It was the first time that Penny was this forward and it shook Alex. It was a new side of her and he loved it. She exuded confidence as she returned his stare.

Alex's hand wandered into her hair and pulled her head back to keep their eyes locked.

"I hope you're ready for what you're unleashing with your seductive hands, Penelope."

"Just stop talking, Alex and fuck me already!"

Alex chuckled at her insistence. She surprised him by lifting over his turgid length and pushing down to impale his hard cock deep inside her. His breath snagged as she tightened the muscles around his pulsing shaft.

"Hmm . . . now what, luv? Now that you've got me where you wanted . . . what . . . ah, fuck, baby," he gasped as Penny lifted herself and with a small cry, began to rock him. He leaned back against the tub, watching as her eyes flared and her breathing escalated.

"Damn, Alex, that feels so good," she wheezed.

The acceleration of his heart rate was indicative of the desire to pound her with all the lust that was raging through him. But he didn't. She had taken the initiative, for the first time, which excited him to no end.

"It sure does, baby," he whispered as he flexed his cock, smiling as she caught her breath.

She pushed down, forcing him in to the hilt, fusing their bodies as one. Alex nuzzled his face between her breasts, lashing at the succulent tips of her nipples with his tongue. Penny responded by clenching herself around his throbbing shaft and rocked against him with long, slow strokes that awakened a hunger for a release only she could offer him.

"Oh god, Alex. I need to . . . I have to . . ."

Penny's body shuddered. She started to ride him, hard and fast, with a wildness that spurred the beast inside him to life.

"Goddamn, Penelope, slow down," he urged, doing his best to keep his rising climax at bay. "Jesus!" He shouted when she reached back and squeezed his balls, hard, and started bucking on top of him.

"No. I'm done with slow. I want it hard and fast, Alex. Give it to me!" Penny demanded in a hoarse cry.

"Remember, my sweet wife, you asked for it," he warned as he clamped his hands around her hips to guide them as he forced her body down and his hips jerked wildly into hers.

Penny's ecstatic moans drifted on the warm breeze toward the gentle ripple of water down below.

He thrust.

He plunged.

Deeper, and then *harder*.

Penny gasped as he increased the pace. Their bodies were on fire, demanding more, until their hoarse cries echoed toward the distant moon. Her eyes rolled back in their sockets as her body writhed violently against him until she erupted with him deep inside her loins.

"Alex!" She screamed his name as pleasure washed over her in tumultuous waves of ecstasy, drowning her in the demand of the climax that took control of their bodies.

Penny wrapped her arms around his neck and hugged him fiercely. Alex didn't protest, only returned the favor. A shuddering sigh exposed his emotional turmoil as it escaped his lips.

He was shattered by the feelings that swirled inside him. For the first time in his life, he felt whole—complete. He was struggling to overcome the overwhelming need to give, to hold and to protect.

Her—only her.

His wife.

You never said anything about going on honeymoon," Penny protested as Alex brought the car to a halt next to a private jet sporting the Allied Group's logo. "I haven't made any arrangements at work."

"A phone call will suffice, Penelope. It's only for three days." He leaned over for a brief kiss. "We'll have a proper honeymoon later but there's no way we're starting our marriage without at least a mini one."

Penny was moved by his thoughtfulness. Not to mention the engaging and sexy wink he offered her.

"I suppose you're right. Three days isn't that much."

Her hungry gaze followed Alex's tall frame as he walked around the front of the car to open the door for her, while the flight attendants carried their luggage to the plane.

"Where are we going?" Penny asked as the plane taxied for takeoff. She'd been told to pack minimum clothing, that's it.

Alex tapped her nose with his index finger. Penny's eyes followed the platinum wedding ring that she had placed on his finger the day before. She'd been amazed that he had insisted on one. It was contradictory to the type of man she'd thought he was. She'd never expected that he would *want* to wear a wedding band.

"Now *that*, my lovely wife, is a surprise."

As soon as the seatbelt sign went off, he led her to a luxurious bedroom toward the back of the plane.

"We didn't get much sleep last night and I for one could do with some shut-eye," he explained as he fell onto the bed. He patted the spot next to him. "Come join me, wife."

She didn't need to be asked twice. His arms wrapped around her as he pulled her against his side.

"Hmm," he sighed as he relaxed into the pillow, his eyes closed. "My wife. I never thought I'd ever say this, but it does have a nice ring to it."

Penny smiled in secret delight. Secure in his arms, she was drowning in the happiness that surged through her in that moment. She snuggled closer and before long, drifted off to sleep.

CHAPTER THIRTEEN

"I've never seen you this happy, Penny. The honeymoon seems to have agreed with you; there's a decided glow on your face," Amber observed. She popped a lemon tart into her mouth as she examined her friend.

"I am." Penny's laugh tingled in the quiet restaurant. It was mid-morning and the restaurant was closed until lunch time. "It was just a short trip but I don't think it could've been any more idyllic."

"Nothing beats the Key West in my opinion." Amber lifted the teapot to fill their cups.

"Alex has the most magnificent beach house on Sunset Key. He spoiled me rotten and it felt . . . you know . . ." Penny's hand fluttered in the air. She took a sip of her tea.

"Like a real marriage," Amber interjected. Her brow furrowed in a frown. The discussion they'd had on the wedding day came back to haunt Amber. She'd encouraged Penny to allow free reign to her feelings but now she was concerned that Penny had opened herself to potential hurt. The money that

Drew had embezzled still loomed in the back of her mind.

"Has the issue with Drew's fraud been resolved?"

Penny swallowed the decadent lemon tart before she responded.

"Not yet. With the wedding and Alex and Blake concentrating on getting the Chinatown project off the ground, it's fallen to the wayside. Although he did mention last night that Mark has made headway with it in the interim. He's got all the necessary documentation ready to approach the off-shore authorities to have the money released."

"You couldn't figure out the safe code?"

Penny shook her head. "It could be a number of things. Our birthdays, wedding day, or maybe the day Gran died . . . I just don't know. Our marriage was too fleeting."

"And his accomplice?"

"Nothing. Whoever it is, they are smarter than Drew. Mark is hoping that once they receive word of the money being released, they'll overplay their hand and expose themselves."

Penny popped another miniature lemon tart into her mouth. "Is this a new recipe?" She asked savoring the zesty tanginess on her palate.

"Yes, and as my official tester, what's the verdict?"

"I love it but please take it away. At this rate I'll finish the entire plate and believe me, my hips can't afford it."

Amber laughingly added two more to Penny's plate; who, with a groan of indulgence, finished them as well.

"So, be honest. What's it like to be Alex's wife?"

Penny wiped her mouth and leaned back against the chair. She appeared thoughtful as she examined her feelings carefully before she responded.

"In comparison to being married to Drew?" Penny shrugged. "In the beginning of our marriage, Drew was different. He was considerate and loving but that didn't last long. Over the past two years I've given it a lot of thought. There was always something in his manner that I couldn't decipher. I suppose that's the reason I was always leery of him and we could never really connect. I was hurt but not all that devastated when his true colors came to light." A tender smile brightened her face. "Alex is different. Nothing is forced. Every action, touch and kiss feel like it comes from deep within, a secret place that not even he understands exists. But . . ." Penny hesitated. Her eyelids fluttered.

"But?"

"Sometimes I sense his hesitation. He has such a tight control over his emotions that I wonder if I will ever be able to reach his heart. Maybe I have been fooling myself; that although he's considerate, attentive and loving, his heart will never be affected."

"And you want it to."

Penny smiled dolefully. "More than anything. Living as man and wife is like a dream come true. It's what I've always imagined married life would be like. And, I can't deny it, Amber. I'm not just in love with Alex. I love him with every essence of my being."

"Excuse me, chef," Craig, one of the sous chefs, interrupted them with an apologetic smile. "We're ready for you, boss."

"I'll be right there." Amber got up and Penny followed suit. "You don't have to go. I won't be long."

"I want to pop in at Alex's office. He and Blake are leaving for a four-day business trip to Florida this afternoon." She winked at Amber. "I want to give him a going away . . . er . . . present."

"Well, look at you! You've crawled out of your conservative shell. You go girl," Amber said gaily. She laughed as Penny's cheeks bloomed red.

"Come for dinner tomorrow. I'm sure Craig can manage for one night without you," Penny invited her as they hugged each other.

"Only if you promise to make your decadent peanut butter brownies for dessert."

"Done. I'll see you then."

Penny waved as she walked through the door and got into her car. She hummed along gaily to the song, 'You're the one that I want', from the movie *Grease,* playing on the radio. She parked her car fifteen minutes later in front of the Columbus Circle building block.

Penny's footsteps were light as she walked into the building. She was oblivious to the admiring looks from passersby as they appreciated the strikingly gorgeous woman in a dark purple mini dress. A spaghetti strap slipped provocatively off one shoulder. She reached up to push it back, her fingers tracing the curve of her shoulders. Her calf muscles tightened and her delicate ankles, sheathed in a pair of Jimmy Choo sling backs, arched with every step.

"Morning Mrs. Sinclair," the gray-haired security guard greeted her. Penny stepped into the elevator he was holding for her and returned his smile as the doors closed.

She examined her reflection with a critical eye, turning this way and that. She tossed back her hair with a decisive flick. She was a different woman. Last night she'd learned how to tease and arouse Alex's primal lusts. A sultry smile blossomed on her lips as she made her way to Alex's office.

Gavin, Alex's assistant was nowhere to be found when she walked into the front office. Alex's office door was slightly ajar. Her steps faltered as she overheard her name being mentioned. She tiptoed closer and mischievously decided to eavesdrop on the conversation between Alex, Blake and Mark.

"When are the two of you going to realize that's never going to happen?" Alex's voice sounded amused.

"Who are you trying to fool, mate? Besides, we've already placed the order for our bikes. This is one bet we aren't going to lose," Mark scoffed.

Bet? What have I got to do with a bet?

Alex laughed dryly. "You've already lost the bet, Mark, my friend."

"How so?" Blake interjected.

"We've been married for two weeks and together for what . . . five, six weeks? And I'm still as unaffected by the delightful Mrs. Sinclair as I was when we first met."

A chill raced down Penny's spine, raking through her entire frame like a knife. She pressed her hand to her mouth.

"Yeah, right," Blake laughed.

"Come now, mates. I can't deny that the sex is beyond magnificent but that's as far as it will ever go. Besides, you seem to forget that the marriage is to appease Zhang Wei Chén and is temporary. As soon as the Chinatown project kicks off and is underway, I have no further need for wedded bliss."

Tears blinded Penny's as she stumbled toward the elevator without her realizing it. Her heart felt like it was beating a mile a minute in an effort to keep her body moving forward. Her chest burned from the repressed sobs as she ran toward her car.

"I've been such a *goddamn fool*! I should've known," she cried in the confines of her car. Her hands were trembling so badly that she couldn't get the car started. Eventually she gave up and gripped the steering wheel in a death grip until her knuckles turned white.

She still felt the pain that had pierced her heart when she'd listened to Alex speak in such a derisive tone, as he belittled their relationship—negating everything she'd believed was developing between them so callously.

"You've been such a fool, Penelope. You're not in Alexander Sinclair's league; you'll never be. You were a fucking idiot to believe otherwise." Her voice sounded bitter, aimed at her own stupidity.

Penny finally managed to gain some semblance of calm to drive home . . . to Alex's home, because if truth be told, it never was *their* home. Not as far as Alex was concerned. The thought devastated Penny. She glanced around the elegant foyer of the house. She'd come to love this house. It had truly felt like home. She'd added some of her own personal touches over the past couple of weeks. Something, she now recalled, had amused Alex but he'd indulged her nevertheless. Now she realized why. He had known it wouldn't be for long.

"Oh, god! The bastard even made me believe he wanted children," Penny was devastated with a sudden realization, now staring back to her. "And I agreed."

He'd whispered the wish for a baby to her on their wedding night. Penny had believed the sincerity in his voice. Now the special memory shattered to smithereens.

"All a fucking ruse! And for what? To clinch the deal with Zhang? How could he be this cruel?"

Penny stumbled up the stairs and fell on the bed. Sobs wracked her body as she finally admitted defeat. Alexander Sinclair had used her, ruthlessly; with no consideration to her feelings or the consequences of his actions. She ultimately gave in to sleep; a fatigued, forlorn sob shuddered through her lips, before dying a slow death.

"Damnit, Penelope! Where the hell are you? Phone me the moment you get this message," Alex barked into the phone. He tossed it on the bed and went to stand in front of the large picture-perfect window. He stared across Miami Beach as he towel-dried his hair. A deep frown made his expression brooding, as dark as a thunderstorm brewing over the ocean.

He'd been calling Penny since their arrival in Florida on Monday night. Worry nipped at him. At first, he'd been concerned that Carver's partner in crime had finally lost all patience in an effort to get to the money. His housekeeper had set his mind at ease. Penny was at home; she just refused to answer any of his calls.

"No, it's something else," he muttered. He threw the towel on the bed and started to dress in a custom-made Savile Row suit in indigo linen that matched his piercing eyes, a white shirt and slim Burberry linen tie in pale turquoise completed his ensemble. He looked striking, polished . . . and worried.

He racked his mind but he couldn't recall any incident that could've upset Penny. They'd made love before he'd left for work on Monday—a very satisfying goodbye to tide over the next four days. He grunted as he remembered her cheeky *boob-flash* as she'd waved him off to work later.

Her confidence had blossomed since their wedding, which was why her sudden icy withdrawal made no sense.

He picked up the phone once again and scrolled to Amber's number. He tapped his finger on the screen, hesitating to make the call. It went against his nature to involve a third person in his private matters. But concern for Penelope was foremost in his mind.

His lips flattened; his expression turned grim, making his chiseled jaw twitch.

"H'lo . . . Alex?" Amber's mumbled in thick, sleepy voice.

Alex glanced at his watch. It was after eight in the morning, hours past when she was usually up and at the restaurant.

"Did I wake you?"

"I'm in Los Angeles for a food festival until Friday, so yeah, I guess I'm a little behind you, time wise."

"My apologies. Had I known, I wouldn't have bothered you this early. For that matter, go back to sleep."

"I'm awake now. You might as well—"

"It's not important. I'm sorry I woke you." Alex ended the call. He ran his hand through his tousled hair. He hadn't had a proper night's sleep since Monday and with the busy schedule and back-to-back meetings they've had the past three days, he was bone-tired. If it hadn't been for the meetings scheduled months in advance, Alex would've been home already.

He strode angrily toward the door.

"Penelope better have a damn good reason for this tantrum." His voice sounded clipped as he walked into the empty elevator to meet Blake for breakfast.

"Penelope!"

Alex's voice boomed through the house the moment he slammed inside. He stood glaring around, listening intently; his legs spread, with his hands low on his hips. Anger was apparent in the tense lines of his shoulders.

He inhaled deeply to calm himself. She was home. He could sense her presence, like he had since the day she'd moved in. Her essence filled every corner of his house.

He looked up the stairs and started making his way toward their bedroom. It was just after five in the afternoon but instinct told him that's where Penelope was.

She was sitting on the bathroom floor with her back pressed against the vanity. Her shoulders were shaking with silent sobs.

"Luv, what's wrong?" Alex rushed forward concernedly and hunched down in front of her. He reached for her hand.

She slapped his hand away, like it was the most offensive thing she's ever seen.

"Don't touch me, you bastard!"

Alex reared back as if she'd slapped his face. When she lifted her head, Alex could see the dark circles under her eyes. She was tense like a cable, stretched too tight and beginning to fray.

"Penelope, what the fuck is going on?" His brow furrowed and his mouth turned grim.

"What is going on? You mean you don't know? I find that hard to believe," she snarled at him. "High and mighty Alexander Sinclair has everyone wrapped around his little finger." She snorted. "You've had it all planned from the beginning, didn't you? Right to the last, minute detail."

Her voice sounded hollow; an explosion of rage that Alex couldn't make sense of, no matter how hard he tried.

"Penelope—"

"Don't *Penelope* me," Penny trembled with anger. She had deliberately avoided his calls to give herself the time to calm down before she had to face him.

Only, she hadn't counted on the devastating discovery she'd just made.

"Tell me, Alexander, just when were you planning to inform me?"

Alex felt a chill fill his veins as her angry gaze sliced through him.

"Inform you of what?" His lips barely moved. His face had turned impassive as he evaluated her hostility.

"That this farce of a marriage was only temporary," she sneered. Her voice thickened as tears of anger threatened to overpower her.

"Sweetie, listen to—"

"Well, congratulations, Sinclair. Your empty promises worked. Your entire plan has come to pass. I'm just sorry I was too enthralled to see through your phony charm." She pushed to her feet. "You've got a wife and now . . ." She slammed her hand against his chest. He automatically grabbed the white plastic stick that bounced off his chest. "You've hit the jackpot. You have a child on the way. All wrapped up in one neat package. The perfect, sweet little family to appease Zhang! Yes, I figured it out! You didn't want a baby with *me* like you oh, so sweetly begged for. It was all business!"

Alex was stumped at the unexpected joy that exploded inside him. A baby! But the joy shriveled under the hate that radiated from her darkened green eyes; fierce and uncompromising.

"I want to know what's going on, Penelope. You're hysterical."

"Yes!" She shrieked. "I am *furious*! I'm waiting, Sinclair." Her tone was raw. "Exactly when were you planning to tell me this marriage is a farce to you. You, who told me you *don't do pretend!* Duh!" She spit out in disgust. "Answer me, damn you! Before or after the baby is born?"

Alex appeared stoic as he stared at her, a heaviness descended upon him.

Penny couldn't detect a sliver of emotion in his cool eyes

"That's what I thought. You were never going to tell me. How did you plan on getting rid of me, Alex? Turn away from me? Have an affair with another woman?" Penny pummeled his chest with her fists. "Tell me, damn you!"

"Where did you hear—"

"From your own lying lips!" She croaked as she finally couldn't hold back the tears any longer. Alex's expression turned somber as she haltingly told him of her intended surprise and what she'd overheard.

"Penelope, it isn't as simple or as straightforward as that."

"Oh, get off it, Alex. I might have been gullible enough to believe that even though we married for unconventional reasons, you'll come to develop feelings for me; that we'll build a life together. But I'm not an idiot; not any longer."

Penny turned to leave but her knees buckled as her body gave in from lack of sleep and nutrition. Alex caught her in his arms and carried her to the bed. She struggled as he followed her down and pulled her into his arms.

"Get your hands off me. I don't want you to touch me," she protested breathlessly.

"Tough. I'm not going anywhere." Alex clamped her arms against her sides and locked his legs around her kicking ones, effectively trapping her in a cocoon.

"Enough, Penelope. You need to calm down."

His arms tightened as she renewed her struggles, until eventually, she gave up from sheer exhaustion. Not long after, she drifted off to sleep.

Alex opened his hand and stared at the white stick in his hand. The pregnancy test. She was expecting his child. He rose on his elbow to stare down at her. She looked fragile, with her lips turned into a vulnerable pout, even in her sleep. He deeply regretted that she'd overheard his callous remarks to his friends. What she didn't know was that it had been a final desperate attempt to keep his heart from completely losing the battle to her allure.

He traced the frown that formed between her brows, his fingers gently brushing over her cheeks and continued the feathery caress over her lips. A soft sigh escaped through them. His gaze lowered. He hesitated only briefly before he pushed her dress up over her hips, baring her stomach. His hand was trembling as he gently covered the natural curve of her belly.

"My child." His voice grated with raw reverence as the reality of the words he'd just uttered hit home. He couldn't contain the elation that ran through him like a beam of sunshine. He leaned down to kiss the satiny softness of her stomach.

"My flesh and blood. Ours!"

Alex lay down again and pulled Penny into the curve of his arm. Her head nestled to find its usual spot on his chest. He drifted off to sleep. A smile curved around his lips. His hand came to rest on Penny's stomach in an unconscious protective gesture.

The next morning, Alex stood staring at Penny who was still sleeping deeply. His sigh dragged out like a never-ending winter. He cursed the fact that he had agreed to an urgent meeting that Zhang had requested yesterday for ten this morning. He and Penny needed to talk but she obviously needed to rest. The tired lines and dark shadows on her face attested to her lack of sleep.

Alex returned home four hours later. The emptiness, when he walked into the house, was like a knife in his gut. He knew it then.

Penny had left him.

Chapter Fourteen

"Alex will hunt you down, you know that, right?" Penny yanked on the cable ties that bound her wrists in front of her. She winced as they cut into her skin.

"Shut your mouth, Mrs. Sinclair. You're giving me a headache."

Penny glowered at the burly man with the big, sloping shoulders. He was pouring a drink for himself.

"Good. I hope your head explodes."

His cold gaze fixed on her with a predator's unwavering attention. He tipped his head back and chucked down the drink.

"So, you're the one," Penny prodded. She glanced around the luxurious study that he'd carried her into. Try as she might, she couldn't envision him as the owner of this place. He was too rough around the edges.

He blithely ignored her as he made a phone call.

"I've got her," his voice clipped through thin lips; his eyes trailed over her body.

Penny pushed herself upright in a defensive gesture, glad that she'd opted for comfortable jeans and a light sweater that morning. She had moved in with Amber three days ago. She'd left Alex's house right after he had on Saturday. She hadn't even cared about the bodyguards following her. She knew she *had* to get away.

She curbed the despondency that always flooded her when she was reminded of her breakdown. She needed time to think. So far, she'd not found a solution to the conundrum she was facing.

She was caught in the middle of a tidal wave. Should she file for a divorce or was there a chance of Alex realizing his mistake and making amends?

The fact that she was carrying his child had been an important factor too. Was it fair to deny her child the love of its father? The security of a family?

"No, she made it easy. She chose to take a cab this morning."

The grating voice of her abductor yanked her attention back to the present.

"Luckily I was there to pick her up." He laughed. "Don't worry, babe, it wasn't the first time I had to shake off somebody. Her bodyguards were easy as a pie. No one knows where she is."

He refreshed his drink, watching Penny through slitted eyes.

"The plane is ready. When do you want to leave?" He nodded and finished his drink. "Good. We'll meet you at the airport." He ended the call and slipped the cell phone into his pocket.

"So, you're not the one. You're just a game piece for someone else. A woman? Your wife?"

"You talk too much," he growled darkly.

"What's your name?"

"None of your concern. Get up. We're leaving," he ordered abruptly. Penny's painful cry echoed in the room as he yanked her up. "Don't test my patience, woman."

"Then let me go, you asshole."

"I suggest you shut that trap of yours. I can always gag you."

Penny decided it was in her best interest to back down and rather concentrate on finding a way to escape. If they were on their way to an airport, it could only mean one thing. They were taking her to the off-shore banks to get their greedy hands on the money. She had to remember it wasn't just her own life at stake anymore. Her unborn child was also at risk.

The hour-long drive, to the Republic Airport on Long Island, was undertaken in complete silence.

Penny's thoughts drifted off to the messages that Alex had left her over the last few days. The one she had received this morning, just before she'd left for work, replayed in her mind.

"Penelope, please answer your phone. Nothing in life is ever just black or white. Please, luv, I need to explain."

The car rocked to a halt and brought her musings to an end. She stared at the private jet in front of the car. She leveled a taunting look at the sour man next to her. "This is a waste of time, Grumpy."

He ignored her and dragged her up the stairs, pushing her through the doorway. The steady hum in the background indicated that the plane had already been warming up. The door closed behind them with a decisive click as he shut off Penny's only escape route.

"Let's get in the air, Captain," Clive said to the pilot who stood watching from the cockpit.

"Right away."

Penny felt despondent as she felt the plane slowly ease forward.

"Come inside and take a seat, my dear," a familiar voice drifted toward Penny. She tentatively walked deeper into the plane.

"*You?*" Penny gawked at the beautiful woman lounging in one of the plush seats. "I *knew* there was something suspicious about you," Penny fumed.

Gabrielle watched Penny with a sardonic smirk on her face. "So much so that you immediately ran to your dear husband and tattled on me? About your suspicions?" She laughed boisterously at Penny's disgruntled expression of self-recrimination; evidence that Penny hadn't mentioned the meeting to Alex. "Yes, I didn't think so. Don't you now wish that you had acted on your first instincts?"

"I repeat what I've been trying to get through Grumpy's thick skull; you're wasting everyone's time. I have no idea what the stupid failsafe code is."

"You're lying," Gabrielle fired back at her. She spread her fingers to admire her long, red fingernails.

"Don't you think if I *did* know, the money would be back where it belongs already?"

Gabrielle snorted. She watched Penny with the predatory look in her eyes. "Alex might be infatuated enough to believe you're innocent. I know better." She leaned forward; she exuded a dangerous quality that warned Penny not to underestimate her. "You're planning to butter him up now that you're married and then you'll claim the money as an added bonus."

"You are truly demented, do you now that? Newsflash, Ms. Brittle, I *have* money. I don't need stolen money."

"Don't fool yourself, Miss Goody-Two-Shoes. No one says no to forty-five-million dollars." She turned to the man next to her. "Did you check if she has her passport in her handbag, Clive?"

"Yes, it's in my pocket."

Penny cursed herself for not removing her passport after the trip to sign the documents at Gabrielle's office. She held out her hands.

"Please, my hands are turning numb." Penny exhaled loudly when Clive just stared at her. "Look, we're thousands of miles in the air. Where am I gonna go?"

"Cut her loose," Gabrielle said and sneered at Penny, "But I'm warning you, don't try anything. Clive won't hesitate to thump you over the head."

Penny didn't respond. She relaxed in the seat, rubbing her stinging wrists while staring out of the small window. Her mind was blank.

"One warning, Penelope. If you truly don't know that code, I suggest you put your brain to work. If you fuck this up, your life is worthless to us. Got it?" Gabrielle's black eyes pierced into Penny's.

"I understand," Penny responded dully. Suddenly, the future ahead was bleak and frightening for her.

Think, Penny! It has to be something that had certain significance to Drew.

Penny wrung her hands together. For the first time in her life, she experienced gut wrenching fear.

Oh god, Alex, find me! You have to realize I've been abducted. Please! For the sake of our child.

"Morning Amber," Alex answered the call despondently. He glanced at his watch. It was already nine in the evening and he was still at work. His stomach growled, reminding that he hadn't eaten since breakfast.

"Is Penny with you, Alex?" Amber asked in a tone that was wrought with concern.

Alex surged upright. A sense of doom careened through him.

"I thought she was with you."

"The last time I saw her, she was getting into a cab from my restaurant to her work. That was at nine this morning."

"A cab?"

Alex checked the messages that Gavin had sent to his email. There wasn't anything from his security team.

"She didn't feel like driving in traffic this morning. She's been suffering from nausea. I've been trying to get hold of her the entire day. At first the calls went to voicemail when she didn't answer but now, it's just turned off."

Alex's violent curse echoed over the airwaves.

"Oh no! Alex, do you think she was kidnapped? For the money?" The fear in Amber's voice echoed his own.

"Let's hope not, Amber. I'll get hold of Mark. We might be able track her phone through his FBI resources."

"Please keep me in the loop, Alex. I don't know what I'll do if something happens to Penny."

"Nothing is going to happen to her, Amber. I promise you, I *will* find her."

Alex contacted Blake and Mark. They arranged to meet at the FBI offices in Manhattan. Mark had already put the technical team to work by the time Alex and Blake arrived.

"We can't log into Penny's current location, but we managed to find the last signal before the phone was turned off." Mark pointed to the map of New York that was on the large screen on the wall.

"The last signal bounced off the cell tower at the Republic Airport on Long Island. I already requested flight plans of all private and corporate planes leaving during that time slot. We should have it in ten minutes."

Alex began to pace back and forth. He felt like a caged lion, helpless but charged with enough energy to go on a rampage . . . a killing one. Of whoever had taken Penny.

"Blake, please contact our pilot to get the plane ready and to log a flight plan to the Caymans," Alex said quietly. Mark and Blake could hear the suppressed violence in his voice.

"On it, mate." Blake immediately made the call while Alex resumed his prowling.

"You do know that Penny's life is in danger, Mark? Especially once they realize that the money has already been returned to us when they get there," Alex voiced the concern that had been running through their minds.

The Director of Public Prosecution (DPP) of the Cayman Islands had instructed the Financial Crimes Unit of the Royal Cayman Islands' Police Service (RCIS) to investigate the forensic proof that Mark had supplied of Drew's embezzlement. The bank had been instructed to release the money into the Allied Group's account three days ago. The same process had reached success with the Swiss Bank too.

"Surely Penny would tell them that the money is no longer there," Blake asserted.

Alex ran a tired hand over his eyes. "She doesn't know." He exhaled slowly and briefly told them what had transpired before Penny had moved out but he left out the news about her pregnancy. "She refuses to take my calls, so I haven't had the opportunity to inform her."

"What a fuckup," Mark said dolefully. He glanced at Blake. Now they understood the reason for Alex's black mood lately.

"Why haven't you gone to talk to her?" Blake asked with a concerned frown.

"She moved in with Amber. I've been there every fucking day, Blake. I can't even get into the goddamned building, the security is so tight, and obviously, Amber refuses to grant me entry."

"Obviously. Those two are close and very protective of each other." Mark murmured. "Thank you, Agent Lucy," He took the report that she handed to him. "No flight plans to Switzerland and there's only one plane that left for the Caymans. It belongs to . . . fuck me." Mark's voice turned gravely as he lifted an angry gaze to his friends. "You're not going to believe this."

"What? Jesus, Mark, stop wasting time," Alex exploded with concern in his eyes.

"The plane is registered to Lowman, Lovett and Brittle, Attorneys at Law."

"Gabrielle Brittle. That fucking bitch!" Alex was livid. "She couldn't seduce me, so she used a weakling like Carver to enrich herself." Alex marched toward the door. "What time are they landing in the Caymans?"

Mark checked the logs and then glanced at his watch. "They landed thirty minutes ago."

"Let's go. At least they won't be able to do anything tonight. Mark, get your team to keep working. We need to know where they went. I doubt they would be bold enough to book into a hotel. They might have rented a cottage or an apartment close to the bank. Although, I think the best strategy would be to wait for them at the bank and catch them red-handed, so to speak."

"I agree, but it will still be good to know where they are and get the local cops to keep an eye on them." Blake followed Alex down the hallway.

Mark snapped orders to his team on the way. "And, Lucy, inform the DPP and the RCIS in the Cayman what's going on. We need their backup when we arrive. Ask them to check video footage at the airport and on street cams. They'll be better equipped to find them than us from here. Call me if you have any information about their location."

Within thirty minutes, they were in the air.

Penny floated on a hazy cloud. She frowned as she endeavored to shake off the last remnants of sleep. Her legs moved listlessly. A soft moan sounded in the room as she snuggled deeper into the soft pillow. She had been overly tired after the flight and because of that she had the first sound sleep in a week. Her heavy limbs and eyelids refused to obey the halfhearted command from her mind to stay awake.

"Time to wake up, sleeping beauty." Gabrielle shook Penny's shoulder rudely.

Penny rolled onto her back. Her eyelids fluttered open as she lazily stretched out, deliberately ignoring Gabrielle who stood next to the bed, watching her.

"Get moving. You have a phone call to make." She sauntered toward the door. "You have ten minutes before I send Clive to come and get you." She glanced at Penny over her shoulder with a taunting look. "And he won't care whether you're dressed or not."

Penny pushed upright as soon as the door closed behind her. After a quick trip to the bathroom, she got dressed in the dark gray pants and apricot colored silk blouse that Gabrielle had left hanging against the closet door. She was brushing her hair when the door opened and Clive walked in.

"Let's go." He didn't bother to hide his irritation.

Penny imagined it had something to do with how Gabrielle had been barking out orders at him and expected him to snap to attention every time. She was waiting for them in the spacious, open-plan living area of the condo they had rented, across the street from the bank.

"Breakfast first." She noticed Penny's surprise as she took in the generously laid out meal on the dining room table. "I'm not inhumane, Penelope. I firmly believe that breakfast is the most important meal of the day. Besides, we don't want your grumbling stomach to draw unwanted attention, now do we?"

Penny sat down and silently buttered a scone. She slathered generous amount of cheese on it and bit into it. She hadn't realized how hungry she was. She just hoped she won't suffer from a bout of nausea, which had been happening every other day lately.

"Not very talkative today, are you, *Mrs. Sinclair.*"

Penny detected a sharp edge in Gabrielle's tone and didn't miss the emphasis she'd placed on Mrs. Sinclair. A brief glance confirmed that she was shooting daggers in Penny's direction. They glowed with signs of jealousy.

Well, well. Ms. Brittle obviously had her sights set on Alex.

The thought settled inside Penny's mind like an awakening boil. It throbbed and irritated her to no end. Just the thought that Alex might have been intimate with this harpy made her want to puke. She wanted to pounce on her and rake her eyes out. She suppressed the desire for violence and continued to eat, choosing not to respond.

"Are you ready for this? You have one chance to supply the correct code."

Penny took another bite; her gaze moved to stare at the ocean through the wall of windows. She'll be damned if she gave Gabrielle the satisfaction of knowing how scared she really was. She finished her breakfast with a glass of freshly squeezed orange juice.

Gabrielle slapped a sheet of paper down on the table.

"This is what you need to say. I'm warning you, Penny, don't deviate from the script. A broken finger or two isn't something you want to suffer while going to the bank."

Penny nodded. If only she could get to her phone. She was praying that it might work but she wasn't sure. All she knew was that one way or the other, she had to find a way to warn Alex. She glanced around furtively. Her handbag was on the small table in entrance hall. Clive had switched off her phone during takeoff but he'd returned it to her bag.

If I could get it out and slip it unobtrusively in my pants pocket—

"Concentrate, Penelope!" Gabrielle snapped as she dialed the bank's number. She pushed the cell phone into Penny's hands. "Stick to the script," she warned her once more.

Penny had no alternative but to follow the order. Gabrielle couldn't hide her surprise when Penny was transferred directly to the bank manager. She'd been dealing with the manager in charge of international deposits and had expected him to be the one to finalize the transaction. Penny didn't miss the worried glance she shared with Clive.

Penny read the script word for word, cognizant of the fact that the phone was on speaker and the two embezzlers were listening in. The manager's responses triggered a feeling of unease in Penny's mind. Something was wrong, or the bank had been instructed to take specific actions. She felt hope bloom inside her. She did her best to keep her expression impassive. It wouldn't do to trigger Gabrielle and Clive's suspicions, who had relaxed the further the conversation progressed.

"Very well, Mrs. Carver. Will eleven o' clock this morning suit you? Unfortunately, I won't be available to assist you until then."

"Eleven is perfect, thank you, Mr. Jones."

Gabrielle gestured furiously, indicating that she should insist on an immediate meeting. Penny ignored her and ended the call.

"What the fuck do you think you're doing?" She flashed a dark look at Penny. "Clive," she snapped as she shifted her angry glare in his direction. He grabbed Penny's hand.

"Noo! Oh god, stop," Penny cried out in pain and struggled violently against his strong grip. "I didn't have a choice! He made it clear that only he can assist me. You heard him! He's only available at eleven."

"Fuck!" Gabrielle pushed back the chair so hard that it clattered to the floor. She looked back as Penny continued to whimper painfully. "Enough, Clive. Let her go."

He dropped her hand with a snort. Penny's eyes turned to dark with pain as she gingerly massaged her abused fingers which Clive had ruthlessly bent backwards.

"Relax, babe, it's only an hour and a half. We're close to walking away with forty-five-million dollars. Let's not do anything rash," Clive cautioned Gabrielle who was pacing back and forth. She kept glancing at Penny; worry apparent on her face.

"I don't like it, Clive. Didn't he sound suspicious to you?"

"You're imagining things, babe. He was only following protocol. Sit down. You're making my head spin."

The time stretched out like a never-ending piece of yarn. Every move Penny made was met with scrutiny and she eventually gave up trying to get to her handbag. She had developed a throbbing headache trying to think of an escape plan. Trying to outrun Clive would be futile; he seemed fit and had proven his mean streak. She couldn't chance anything that would put her baby at risk. She raked a disdainful glance at Gabrielle.

"Why?" She couldn't keep the question back any longer.

Gabrielle shot a hawkish look toward Penny. "I would've thought it's obvious. Alexander Sinclair owes me."

"For what? He trusted you; otherwise he would never have appointed you as the company's legal advisor."

"You don't get it. Why be satisfied with a couple of million dollars a year, which I have to work my ass off for, by the way, when I can have more than I could spend in a lifetime?" She shot Penny an acrimonious look. "And I was on the verge of hitting the jackpot when you appeared on the scene."

"Me? What do I have to do with it? The money had already been stolen by the time I met Alex." Penny frowned as she tried to make sense of Gabrielle's mutterings.

"I had it all planned out. Alex would've fallen for my charms and he was well on the way too. We've had a couple of very, shall I say, satisfying interludes over the past year. He was supposed to marry me. Not you!"

Penny's eyes widened. "You stole from him. What made you think he would ever forgive you for that?"

"He would never have known if Drew hadn't wound up dead. I have proven my worth and I'm just as successful as Alex. I am a perfect match for him."

"What the fuck are you saying, Gabrielle?" Clive ranted. "What about me? Where the hell do I figure in this harebrained scheme?"

Gabrielle continued, hardly taking note of Clive's fury. "Then I would've had billions. *Billions!* But no, he had to go and get married to a little mouse like you. Ugh! I want to puke just thinking about it."

"You have lost your mind, Gabrielle," Penny said with a sad smile.

That triggered the violence that had been shimmering in Gabrielle's eyes. She pounced on Penny and fisted a hand around a tuft of Penny's hair and yanked back her head.

"Aaww, Jesus!" Penny screamed. It felt like she was tearing her scalp.

"Don't you fucking judge me. I am better than you and you will never understand what drives me," she spat into Penny's face. "You better watch your step, Penelope. My patience has run out."

She straightened and recommenced her pacing. Penny wiped away the tears that had sprung to her eyes and rubbed her scalp, watching Clive's furious expression.

"You planned to marry Sinclair? What did you intend to do with me, Gabrielle," he bit out again. "Don't fucking ignore me, bitch!" He grated through clenched teeth. Penny could see he was on the edge of exploding.

Gabrielle turned to him. She cupped his chin and smiled seductively. "Come now, Clive. You know there will always only be you in my heart but Alex would've paved our future. I never intended the marriage to last; just a couple of years until I moved some of his assets over to my name. Relax, honey. Besides, it's all a moot point now, isn't it?" She leaned closer and locked her lips to his in a brief but obviously passionate kiss. "It's time to go," she said with a sweet smile as she stepped back. "Bring her."

Clive seemed appeased as he dragged Penny to her feet. He pushed his face into hers and flayed her with a look of cruel intent. "Put one foot wrong, say one word you shouldn't, and you won't see the sunrise tomorrow. Are we clear?"

"Yes," Penny responded, not bothering to hide the contempt in her response, although she knew he posed a real threat.

Clive kept his vice-like grip around Penny's elbow as they briskly walked across the street toward the bank. He kept glancing around; his body taut as a guitar string.

The heat and humidity were oppressing and clamped down on Penny. The cool interior of the bank was refreshing as they walked inside. A gust of air lifted the damp hair off Penny's temples. She was on the edge. She still had no idea what code to use but hoped once she knew how many digits were required that she'd be able to figure it out.

They were directed to a small conference room to await Anton Jones.

"Remember Penelope, I'm here as your legal counsel and Clive is your brother."

"I'm not an idiot, Gabrielle. I don't need to be reminded six times."

"Careful, Penelope, you're not home free yet," she warned with a grim look on her face.

The evil grin on Clive's face reawakened the fear that Penny had been trying to subdue. She wasn't naïve enough to believe they would allow her to go free once they had the money. She was a liability—an eye witness to their crime.

Think Penny! You have to find a way to get away from them before leaving the bank, otherwise . . .

The door opened and Anton Jones stepped inside. He smiled as he held out his hand to Penny. "Mrs. Carver, you certainly resemble the photo we have on our system. Welcome to the Cayman Islands."

Penny's smile was stiff when she introduced Gabrielle and Clive.

"Can I offer you some refreshments? Coffee, tea, perhaps?" He asked with an engaging smile.

"No, thank you. If you don't mind, we are in a bit of a hurry. Our flight is leaving this afternoon."

Clive took the initiative to respond when Penny kept quiet.

"Of course." Anton opened the folder he had carried in with him and requested to see Penny's passport. He verified the authenticity and handed it back to her with a nod. "So far so good." He got up and gestured toward the door. "The final verification instructions are in a safety deposit box. Please follow me."

Penny's eyes flashed left and right as they walked, desperately searching for an opportunity that could aid in her escape. It was another foiled attempt as they stepped inside the secure vault.

"Mrs. Carver, your thumb print is required to unlock the locker, please." Anton pointed out the box and explained the process.

The locker door flicked open, at the same time, the door behind them opened. Penny glanced over her shoulder.

"Alex!" She breathed in agonized relief.

"RCIS! Everybody stay where you are." An authoritative voice boomed in the enclosed room.

Before anyone could react, Clive wrapped his arm around Penny's neck and held her as a shield in front of him. His hold tightened around her throat as she began to struggle. She gasped for breath as he brutally cut of her air supply.

"Let her go." Alex's voice sounded hoarse and far away as she struggled to draw a breath.

"Stay away! I'm warning you, if anyone touches me or Gabrielle, I'll snap her neck," Clive bellowed. His body was taut, warning off the advancing officers.

"He will too," Gabrielle said in a breathless voice. She had gone as pale as a sheet.

"Move! All of you, toward the back of the room. Now!" Clive barked the order, tightening his hold again when Alex hesitated. Penny clawed at his arm as her vision was filled with black dots.

"Al-ex, pl-ease," Penny begged in a muffled squeak, her eyes as big as saucers.

"Do as he says," Alex clipped, his voice filled with dark rage. His eyes met Penny's. "Stay calm, luv. Take short, shallow breaths and try not to panic," he said in a deep, soothing voice. It immediately calmed her down.

Penny's eyes were glued to him. He had never looked more endearing than he did in that moment of anguished terror.

Clive hedged toward the door, his warning glare anchoring the three police officers and Alex to the spot. "Do not fucking move. If anyone follows us, I'll kill her."

"Al-ex," Penny croaked, wracked with fear that it could be the last time she would see him.

Clive slammed the door shut, breaking their eye contact.

"Move, babe," Clive urged Gabrielle who seemed unsure of herself for the first time since Penny had met her. "Down the side hallway, we'll leave through the staff entrance." Clive instructed her with a gruff voice.

Gabrielle changed direction and rushed down the narrow hallway.

"Let me go," Penny pleaded, finally able to breathe since Clive's hold on her had eased.

"Shut up, bitch." His voice sounded surly. "Faster, babe. We've got to get the fuck out of here," he urged Gabrielle. For the first time, cracks of panic were showing in his demeanor.

"Fuck! We need an employee access card to unlock the door, Clive!" Gabrielle wailed.

Clive pushed a plastic card into her hand. "I picked Jones'."

Gabrielle swiped the card and the door clicked open. She ran outside, with Clive yanking Penny along.

Then all hell broke loose.

"Noooo! Let me go," Gabrielle's scream sounded like a wailing hyena in the wild.

Penny acted instinctively and kicked back, the heel of her shoe connecting directly with Clive's knee. He howled and lost the hold he had on her. Penny tried to scramble out of his reach but his fist closed around her hair and he yanked her back.

"Argh!" Penny screamed in pain as her ankle twisted and she fell to the ground, hitting her head against the wall.

"Don't move!" Penny recognized Mark's voice as she fought against the black void that threatened to swallow her whole.

"Come on you fucker! Do it. Give me a reason," Mark bellowed as Clive twisted around to run.

Penny squinted and tentatively probed the painful throb on the side of her temple.

"Oh god," she whimpered as pain shot through her brain. She was appeased only slightly when she watched Mark cuff Clive's hands behind his back.

"Penelope!" Alex's deep voice penetrated through the haze that she was struggling to shake off.

"Alex," she managed to croak. Then he was there. His arms folded around her as he gently lifted her on his lap. Penny clung to his arms.

"My head! Oh god, it hurts," she moaned as a fresh wave of pain caused tears to fill her eyes from the sudden movement. She stared at him, never having seen him so angry. He looked volcanic—ready to erupt as he traced her cheeks.

"I've got you, luv. It's all over. Just relax, baby. I've got you."

Alex held her tight against his chest. His heart pounded as she leaned against him. The blaze in his eyes sharpened on the growing lump on her temple. He had a hard time keeping his anger in check. He would love nothing more than to choke that fucker with his bare hands. But Penny needed him now. His eyes softened as realization hit.

But not as much as I need her.

"I want to go home," Penny sounded extremely tired.

"Yes, my love, we're going home."

Penny's mind wrapped around the words 'my love'. She held her breath as she searched his gaze, feeling the swirling darkness slowly invading her mind. She shook off the need to slip into oblivion. If only it was the truth but it was more likely a figment of her imagination in a moment of pain-induced wishful thinking.

"Thank you," she whispered.

"For what, luv?"

"For coming for m-e." The cruel hammering pain inside her head became unbearable. Shadows crawled closer, darkening the outer edges of her vision. They shrouded her mind in a black void and flung her into oblivion.

Alex gently brushed back her hair. He placed a tender kiss on her forehead and whispered against the familiar fragrance of her skin, "Yes, my love, we're going home."

CHAPTER FIFTEEN

"You are *not* going back to your apartment, or to Amber's, Penelope, and that's final."

"The danger is over. Drew's accomplices are behind bars and your money is back where it belongs. I am no longer your responsibility, Alex."

Alex's expression turned bilious for a fleeting moment before the usual impassive mask fell into place.

"You forget that you're carrying my child."

Penny's shoulders pulled back, forming a straight line; her eyes clouded with anger.

"Believe me, it's something I'm not likely to ever forget."

Alex was shaken by the chips of emerald ice that turned Penny's eyes into chilled glaciers. He gritted his teeth, his voice turning guttural.

"Do you resent the baby, Penelope?" His voice was doused in bleak dejection.

Penelope couldn't tear her eyes from his. His penetrating look pierced through every layer of self-preservation she had erected around her emotions since they'd left the Cayman Islands.

"The baby is the only saving grace in this mess, Alex. I could never hate it."

She ran her hand through her hair. The heavy sigh swirled through the air and sounded like she was carrying the weight of the world on her shoulders.

"But that doesn't mean that I'm prepared to bring my child into a world of lies and deceit."

"What are you saying?"

"I'm saying I'm leaving, Alex. A child is a gift to two people who love each other, not a tool in a corporate project."

"Penelope—"

"No. I will *not* allow you to use my child, Alex. I'm afraid you'll have to find another way to appease Zhang Wei Chén."

Penny started toward the door. Alex was there before her, blocking her way.

"You're not going anywhere. At least not until I've had the opportunity to explain."

"Alex . . ." Penny's shoulders hunched forward. Weariness and fatigue closed in on her. She could feel her legs beginning to tremble. "Very well, but not tonight. I'm dead on my feet." She walked toward the stairs. "I'm going to sleep." She shot him a hot-tempered look over her shoulder. "I trust you'll honor my desire to be left alone."

Alex watched her gently swaying hips as she climbed the stairs until she disappeared from view.

"Jesus, what a mess," he muttered under his breath.

Her frailty tugged at Alex's heart. He flinched at the memory of the helplessness he'd felt when that bastard Clive had threatened her life.

He found solace in his study as he settled behind his desk and stared into the darkness that surrounded him. The memory of how weak and pale she had been, blared like a trumpet in his mind. His throat closed up and he found it was impossible to breathe all of a sudden.

"Get a grip, Sinclair!"

He inhaled deeply. He focused his mind on the vision of her that always gave him solace—the vision of Penny walking toward him in her flowing wedding dress. A feeling of serenity swept over him, to soothe the choppy sea of emotions that had been threatening to swamp him. Alex brushed a hand over his eyes. Fatigue of the past week caught up with him. It was no use trying to deny it any longer. Penelope had managed to pierce the part of him that had been impenetrable his entire adult life.

His heart.

"Alex?" Penny called his name as she walked down the hallway, surprised to find that he wasn't anywhere to be found. She'd expected that he would corner her first thing this morning.

With a stolid expression she made her way downstairs.

What's going on in that mind of yours, Alex? Or is this another mind game you're playing with me? To keep me on edge?

She reached the ground floor at the same time as the front door was flung open. She relaxed when she realized it was Amber, arriving like an unexpected flash flood. Her eyes brightened when she noticed Penny.

"Oh, thank god you're okay." She caught Penny in a tight embrace, unashamedly crying with relief, which triggered a fresh bout of tears from Penny as well.

"I've never been so scared, Amber. I can't tell you how good it feels to be back home."

Amber leaned back and searched Penny's expression through tearful eyes.

"Are you, Penny? Home? Here?"

"Ugh! I don't know, Amber. I'm so confused." She rubbed her forehead with weary resignation. "I'm famished. Let's get some breakfast."

"Oh no, you don't. I'm the chef, I'll cook," Amber asserted when Penny started gathering eggs and vegetables. She pushed Penny toward the high stools at the breakfast nook. "Sit down, you look pale." She gingerly touched the swollen purple bruise on Penny's temple. "It looks painful."

"It's better than last night, although I still have a slight headache."

Amber quickly brewed some tea and handed Penny a steaming cup before she started chopping vegetables and whisked the eggs. "Vegetable frittata sound good?"

"Heavenly. No one can make them like you."

Penny slowly sipped her tea as she watched Amber's economical movements, preparing their meal.

"He called me, 'my love'," she mused in between sips.

Amber glanced at her. Penny was fiddling with her hair—a sign that she was insecure.

"Do tell."

Penny briefly told Amber what had happened after Gabrielle and Clive had been captured.

"How did it make you feel when he said those words?"

"It was like a caress to my soul," she said candidly. "It's just . . . I think in that moment of relief

249

that it was all over, and the excruciating pain in my head, I might have imagined that he'd said it. You, know . . . wishful thinking that he did care for me and thought of me as his love."

"How sure are you that it was your imagination?"

"Because, he's back to his old ways since our return."

"And that's why you're still here with him in his house?"

"He refuses to let me go until he's had a chance to explain."

"Are you going to listen to Alex, Penny? I mean *really* listen?" She spoke in a quiet, placating tone.

Penny stared at her with a question mark between her brows. "What do you mean?"

Amber popped the pan in the oven to finish off the frittata. She leaned her hip against the counter.

"A man like Alex doesn't wear his feelings on his sleeve, Penny. Nor is he the kind of man who would admit any vulnerability. With him, you need to listen to the meaning behind the words. Remember that when you talk to him."

Penny pondered over Amber's words, not surprised that she had such insight into Alex's character. She'd always had the ability to read what was behind the masks people presented to the world.

"I will. If only I knew what to expect." Her voice thickened as her breath got caught in her throat. "I'm not sure I have the strength for another rejection."

Amber hugged her briefly. "Somehow, I don't think that's a possibility, girlfriend. Trust yourself. I know how devastated you were when you overheard his conversation with Blake and Mark but it might be worth it to give Alex the benefit of the doubt. I believe there is a different side to the story."

"You're right—as always."

"Of course, I am." Amber removed the pan from the oven and heated up their plates before she dished up. "Now, eat up. Little munchkin must be starving."

Penny picked up her fork and froze. She felt his presence without hearing a sound. The air began to sizzle around her, causing her skin to tighten in anticipation. His warmth permeated her skin as he came to stand behind her. Her breath wheezed from her lips as he gently brushed her hair back over her shoulder. His finger left a scorching line on her skin as he traced her cheek.

"Morning, Alex. Are you joining us for breakfast?" Amber asked with a bright smile. She fetched another plate without waiting for his response.

Alex brushed a brief kiss against the bruise on Penny's temple. His breath heated up the chill in her veins.

"Don't mind if I do." He placed a pink confectionary box on the counter. "As long as we can have these chocolate croissants for breakfast I just picked up."

Penny's mouth watered at the sight of the freshly baked delicacies—her favorite. She tingled with pleasure at the thought that he'd specially drove to the bakery ten miles away to spoil her. She sniffed the air appreciatively.

"Nothing beats the smell of freshly-baked chocolate croissants early in the morning," she crooned, ecstasy spreading over her face as she picked one from the box. She did her best to avoid Alex's eyes, somewhat overwhelmed at the tenderness she detected in his eyes.

"Thank you," she mumbled, licking her fingers. Her gaze got snared by Alex's. His eyes dropped to her mouth, watching with a hunger that caused Penny's loins to clench in response.

"I've . . . ahem," Alex had to clear his throat when his voice came out in a hoarse croak. "I've placed a standing order at the bakery. They'll deliver freshly-baked goodies every morning." He finally managed to drag his gaze from her pouty lips and started loading his plate.

Penny gaped at him. "Every morning? Goodness Alex, do you want me to roll down the stairs?"

He whipped an appreciative glance over her trim body, dressed in skinny jeans and a striped cotton shirt.

"You'll never get fat, luv, you're too active. Even if you did, you will always be the most beautiful woman in my eyes."

His earnest response caught her off guard. A blush blooming over her cheeks, betrayed her pleasure at the compliment.

"Have you seen an OB, Penny?" Amber asked, who seemed to have missed the intimate byplay between the two while she was tidying up.

"I have an appointment tomorrow." From her peripheral vision, she noticed Alex's shoulders pull back in a taut line. She looked at Amber with uncertain eyes, who responded by rolling eyes at her. Penny refrained from returning the favor.

If she wanted Alex to be a part of their child's life, now was the time to reach out.

"I've been meaning to ask you but with what had happened . . . the appointment is at eleven, Alex. Will you be able to join me?"

Penny held her breath. She watched him turn his head. She was caught in the moment as she drowned in the warmth that burst to life in his eyes. She had never seen an expression of such radiance on his face. It was humbling and caused a deep crack in the wall around her heart.

"Nothing will keep me away, my sweet." His voice was thick and his Adam's apple rolled up and down as he swallowed the lump in his throat.

Alex finished his breakfast and then pushed off the high barstool. He placed a warm kiss on Penny's cheek.

"Unfortunately, I have to go to the office but I will be home by three this afternoon."

He hesitated and regarded her silently. Her beauty, as always, stunned him but it was more than that. Her soul was pure and it had chipped away his resistance from day one. She did something to him that he was still trying to assimilate.

"Will you be here when I return?" He asked, uncaring that his own insecurity showed in his voice.

To Penny, it sounded like a silent plea. For the first time, a sliver of hope flashed inside her. She offered him a tremulous smile while the cogs in her brain scrambled to connect all the conflicting emotions in her mind.

"I'll be here."

CHAPTER SIXTEEN

Her legs were folded under her. The pale curve of her slender neck was exposed as she played with the silky strands of the long hair cascading like a luxurious curtain down her back. A smile of contentment played around her lips. She'd never looked more beautiful to Alex, who was leaning against the arched entrance of the den. Her lips pursed into a round 'O' as she read something that made her eyes widen. As if sensing his presence, her eyes flickered; her hand stopped its twirling movement. She glanced up.

In that instant he experienced such an emotional connection; he could only stare at her. It was a moment of serenity, where the thin emotive thread that stretched across the short distance, began to rebuild the bridge that had crumbled between them. Alex desperately prayed she would meet him halfway.

He couldn't deny that she had toggled something loose deep inside his soul. It was so intense that he knew he had to act upon it. Life had been bleak since she'd walked out on him. It wasn't the kind of life he wanted to live. Not without her in it.

"I didn't hear you arrive," Penny lilted in a soft voice.

Alex pushed away from the wall and approached her slowly.

"What are you reading?" He gestured at the iPad on her lap.

"A book called *First-time pregnancy*." She smiled whimsically. "There's so much I didn't know. Do you realize that at this point, our baby is the size of a pea and that it'll double in size within a week?"

Alex sat down on the coffee table in front of the sofa. He took the iPad from her and silently paged through the book.

"You never told me how far along you are," he said in a thick voice that was laden with emotion.

"I guess it happened on our first night together. By my calculation I'm six-weeks along."

"Sometimes, well laid plans tend to backfire. Especially the ones made for the wrong reasons." Alex's voice was deep and hollow as it drifted to Penny.

She examined his somber expression as he continued to read the book. He glanced at her. Penny was taken aback by the self-castigation that flashed over his face.

"I stopped believing in love and happily-ever-after, ever since I had to listen to my mother cry herself to sleep over a man who walked away from us. Without giving us a reason, no excuse . . . nothing. He just . . . left." His eyes were dull and lifeless. "The same man had declared his undying love to my mother more times than I could remember."

Alex seemed to be lost in another dimension, another world, where he was ensnared by painful memories. It didn't slip Penny's attention that he didn't call the man 'father', although, she knew that's who he was referring to. The haunting look on his face, of a young boy desperately trying to fill the void, tore at Penny's own heart.

"How old were you?" Penny asked in quiet voice.

"I had just turned nine." He sighed heavily and handed back the iPad to Penny. He tangled his fingers in a fist between his legs.

"For years we lived in limbo. My mother couldn't overcome the heartache and the loss. I believe that's what eventually killed her. She died of grief."

Alex's voice had a rough, raw quality that seared into Penny's soul. She ached to reach out and touch him but his chiseled jaw warned her off.

257

"I was fourteen when I stood next to her grave and felt nothing but relief that she was gone. I loved my mother, dearly, but since *he* left, I had to fulfill the role of the adult in the house. She had become a living ghost. She was suffering in a hell of her own making. As I watched her coffin lower into the ground, I swore that I would never allow my heart to be ruled by emotion—any emotion—least of all love."

He lifted tortured eyes at Penny. "You have to understand, my sweet. I lived with my mother's grief, her heartache and I was forced to experience it with her—every damn day for five years. Living like that for years . . . it hardened me as a young boy." He shrugged negligently. "I hid it well. Charm came naturally to me and I used it to hide the emptiness inside me from everyone. I was content with physical gratification."

His voice trailed off; the conclusion of the man he'd become was inescapable. His shoulders hunched like an old man. His brow furrowed as his mouth turned grim. When he spoke again, his voice rasped with a rawness that echoed the despair in his heart.

"Emotions never crossed my mind when I made that proposal to you. I was physically attracted to you and I knew I would be able to use my experience to my advantage. I thought I could get away with it." His sighed in the silence. "I've always wanted children though; I just didn't want the wife and the emotions that went along with it." He rubbed his eyes. "Fuck, listen to me . . . I never realized how cold and callous I'd become."

"Alex—"

"In my mind, having a child with you would've been my only opportunity of becoming a father."

His expression was forlorn as he stared at her. He knew that he needed to tread very carefully if he wanted their relationship to work and not shatter to pieces.

"Except, you affected me in ways I have never experienced. Fuck, didn't understand. Maybe that's why I didn't tell you the entire truth—that our marriage was supposed to be temporary."

"Supposed to be?" Penny asked with bated breath.

He blinked. The penetrating blue of his eyes held her hostage with a magnetism that had always made her knees weak.

He reached up to caress her cheek. His smile was tender and filled with such warmth that her heart started to beat frantically against her chest. He leaned closer and pressed his lips to hers. The kiss they shared was one of companionship, mutual respect and finally of the warmth that, Penny could only hope, reflected what he felt in his heart. He drew back and dropped his hands between his legs again.

"Something held me back, something that I wasn't ready to admit to myself. We had just met and we didn't know each other very well and yet, I experienced a possessiveness that was completely foreign to me. But, there was more—a feeling that shocked me; that I didn't understand or had any idea how to cope with."

"And that was?" Penny asked breathlessly.

"*Belonging.* No matter how confusing it was, for the first time since he had walked out on us, I felt like I belonged somewhere . . . with you."

He moved to sit next to her. His lips turned up in a brief smile. He took her trembling hands in his. His strong fingers traced the ring on her finger.

"One thing I've come to realize over the past couple of weeks is that the real beauty of life lies in the fact that it's unpredictable. The world evolves every day, bringing with it something new. Everything changes and nothing is permanent. I'm hoping that we can grow together through the changing seasons of life, Penny."

He turned pensive. His gaze remained on their hands, circling her ring.

"That day in my office . . . what you overheard was a desperate attempt to hold on to a promise a young boy had made to himself and a man who has no idea what love is." His fingers tightened around hers as his voice lowered into a soft whisper. "And maybe I never will."

His throat clogged up and he had to swallow hard before he could continue.

"All I know is that I can't imagine what my life would be like without you in it. My bed has been cold and empty since you left. I don't know how to fall asleep, Penelope, without your warm body filling my arms, your gentle breathing lulling me to sleep. In a short period of time, you have become the most important aspect in my life, a vital part of what keeps me sane."

"With him, you need to listen to the meaning behind the words." Amber's advice echoed through Penny's mind. A feeling of serenity flowed through her. Peace, acceptance and love. This was where she wanted to be; where she belonged.

In his arms.

"I don't want our marriage to end, Penelope. I want our little girl to grow up here, in this house, basking in our love and protection." His face contorted in a grimace of wretchedness. "I will devote my life to you and our children, but I can't promise you love, no matter how desperately I'd like to. I can only hope."

Penny beamed with an ebullient smile that made her eyes shimmer like emeralds. She had *listened* and she had heard. Joy filled every molecule in her body. She cupped his cheeks. She placed a feathery kiss on his lips.

"I have enough love for both of us, honey. Whether or not you believe it exists, know that I love you with a depth that I never thought possible. You're it for me. I know that my heart has found a home forever. The rest of my life begins and ends with you. I love you, Alex."

Alex stared at her. Then he smiled gently and leaned in to kiss her. It was a meshing of passion and need. His heart pounded due to emotions that he couldn't decipher but strangely, this time he didn't push them aside. It was time to learn what it could bring.

"Are you sure, luv? Because you have to know, if you give me your heart, no matter how selfish it is, I will never let you go."

"You've had my heart from the beginning, Alex. I tried to deny it at first but when I looked into your eyes as I walked down the aisle, that's when I knew."

"You are such an amazing woman, Penelope. You've made me feel things I find impossible to understand," he said in a raw voice. "But now, I'm not afraid of them. Not with you by my side."

He folded her in his arms and pulled her into a protective cocoon. Her familiar scent drifted into his nostrils as he buried his face in her fragrant hair. His smile exuded tenderness as he untangled her arms from around his neck to look into her eyes.

"You are so beautiful. So pure and to me, a gift that never stops giving. Our journey has only just begun, my love, and I can't wait to unwrap your lovely heart and soul."

Penny peaked shyly at him, her smile bright and so beautiful it stole Alex's breath.

"You said . . . do you want a little girl?"

"No, luv, that's not it. I *know*," he placed his hand on stomach, "I know our little poppet is a little girl."

His lips began a hot trail of nibbling kisses along her collarbone. Before she knew it, he had divested them of their clothes. She stared at the clothing scattered all over the floor in his haste to get them naked.

Her eyebrow arched in a sensual invitation.

"What are you doing, Sinclair?" She pretended to ask in a serious tone then giggled when he pushed her down onto the sofa to settle between her thighs.

"You have to ask, my sweet?" He drawled as he spread her legs wider apart.

Her carnal moan echoed in his ears when he pushed his cock, slowly, but firmly forward, until he was fully encased within her delightful satiny folds. Her pussy embraced every inch of his hard length. Penny arched her back, exulting in the fullness of his throbbing shaft.

"That's the best feeling ever, luv. You, hugging me tighter than a glove."

He dragged her hands over her head to weave their fingers together as he pinned her gently to the sofa. His eyes bore into hers as he pulled back and slowly grinded his turgid arousal deep into her with steady rhythmic thrusts.

"Alex, you feel so good. I missed you, I missed this," Penny moaned between choppy breaths.

He breathed in harshly as their passion consumed him. Penny released a fervent moan as her hunger for Alex subsumed her. He plunged into her, thrusting harder, to the hilt, annihilating any doubts that she might have had of the effect she had over him.

He had an urgent desire to obliterate the painful memory of his unforgiving actions from her mind.

He growled low in his throat when Penny wrapped her legs high around his waist, tilting her hips in a trusting gesture of a selfless offering. He grunted as that small act nearly robbed him of his control. He slumped on top of her, breathing harshly as he fought to bring his rampaging lust under control.

"Easy, baby. Let's not rush this," he breathed against her throat. It was a special moment of reconnecting and it shouldn't be a rushed chase to the end. She deserved more.

Penny trembled as he tightened his fingers around her hands. Her body demanded that he hurry, begging for release. Their eyes caught as he began to stroke his cock into her with a slow, steady rhythm. He noticed her pupils dilating; he heard her breath rush as the involuntary spasms had her pussy clench around his hard shaft. He increased the pace with the knowledge that she was on the edge of a climax. He powered into her, lost in the moment were the world threatened to crash around them. Their cries sounded through the room, which neither bothered to tamper as they both gave in to the passionate demand of their bodies. They erupted with a ferocity that shook them to the core.

"Oh, god, Alex!" Penny puffed, desperately trying to breathe.

"Indeed, my love," Alex echoed as they became lost together, swirling in a wave of bliss so intense, they could do no more than just wallow in the luminescence that left them frail and shattered.

EPILOGUE

The Claimed Bride, a luxurious yacht, in the North Pacific Ocean, one hundred miles east of Maui, Hawaii. Four weeks later.

"This was such a wonderful surprise, honey, although I didn't expect a three-week luxury cruise on this gorgeous yacht." Penny eased into the Jacuzzi on the upper deck and relaxed. Her eyes drifted over the gently rippling ocean that surrounded them.

"We had to christen our boat, luv. It's tradition. A maiden voyage to an exotic location," Alex said as he joined her and lowered himself beside her.

Her eyes twinkled as she glanced sideways at him. "The Claimed bride? That's the best name you could come up with?"

Alex didn't respond but moved between her legs.

"Hmm," Penny sighed as she watched his head lower to place loving kisses all over the slight bulge of her tummy.

"Alex, stop! You can't . . . someone will see us!" Penny shrieked as he quickly removed her bikini top. "Oh . . . hmm," Her protest died in a delightful sigh as she gave herself over to the tantalizing caress of his wicked fingers, gently brushing over her nipples. "What if someone sees us," she purred as she arched her back.

Alex chuckled, his breath hot against her aching nipples. "We're in the middle of the ocean, luv. There's no one around for miles."

His lips wrapped around a nub and he gently sucked it into his mouth. His tongue swirled around the tip while his fingers tugged on the other.

"I have something to ask you," he said as he released her nipple with obvious reluctance. His voice vibrated against her sensitive skin.

"Hmm . . . now? Can't it wait?" Penny sensually pressed her hot core against the hard ridge resting between her legs.

"Nope, can't wait. It has to be now."

Penny shrieked and anchored her arms around his neck as he lifted her in his arms and stepped out of the tub. He placed her on one of the chaise lounges and quickly toweled them dry.

"There, all dry and rosy." His eyes moved with reverence over her body. He couldn't resist leaning down to wrap his lips around her nipple and sucked gently once again.

"I love these babies. Have I ever mentioned that?"

"Once, but you sure show me often enough. Not that I'm complaining, mind you," she said on a quick exhale. Her breath hitched in her throat as she watched Alex go down on one knee.

"Alex?"

He took her hand and pressed a warm kiss in her palm. His smile was warm but had an endearing, boyish quality that tugged at her heartstrings.

"You came into my life at a time I was searching for something to give meaning to my existence. Something to anchor me and give me hope. I never expected the impact you would have on me. You made me whole, my love. You've taught me what it's like to *feel*. I don't know if what is in my heart is love. I *do* know that I have feelings for you that make me feel alive. It has kept me from sinking back into the same quagmire of emptiness that has ruled the majority of my life."

He placed the softest kiss against her lips.

"I realize now that your love has been my savior. The thought of losing you stops my heart. I'm working on learning to understand the emotions raging inside me and that keeps me evolving. I'm a better man when I am with you. You, my gorgeous wife, and your selfless love, taught me that."

Penny blinked back the tears that threatened. Her heart was bursting with love and joy.

"Alex—"

"Penelope Sinclair, would you do me the honor of becoming my wife? To have and to hold from this day forward, for better, for worse, for richer, for poorer, in sickness and in health, to love and to cherish, till death do us part."

Penny couldn't stop the flood of tears, no matter how hard she tried. She smiled through watery eyes at him.

"Honey, we're already married."

"We got married for the wrong reasons, my love. It's time to fix that. I want you to know that although I claimed you as my bride, you have laid claim to my heart. It's yours, my beautiful wife, if you want it."

Penny's blinding smile could have lit a thousand candles.

"Yes, Alex. I will be your claimed bride . . . again."

Claimed Bride

Excerpt: Caught in Between

Book 1 in The Caught Series
Chapter One

"Who in the devil came up with this *brilliant* idea?"

Dax Kaplan thundered, aggravation stark in his voice. His ice blue eyes drilled into those belonging to his COO, Michael, who was standing beside him. Then, with a sardonic twist on his lips, his eyes scrolled down the body of the woman standing before him. The look on his face was a clear indication of his opinion of her.

Venita Baxter's perfectly curved eyebrows rose over her flashing, dark green eyes. She glanced toward Jack Sands, her partner in Black Star Security Services, who frowned at her *'I told you so'* look. Between the two of them, he was the serious one and she was the fun one. Or so he claimed.

She shrugged, turned away on her black, peep-toe Louboutin's and strolled to the far wall, which was covered in photographs. Dax's eyes followed the beautiful brunette in the black dress, which molded to her body, ending just above her knees. The bodice of the dress had white insets that crossed over her breasts, emphasizing her shapely curves. She carried herself with ease and sophistication, with an edge and a unique twist that he could only describe as sensual innocence.

She was a sensationally beautiful woman with a square face in perfect symmetry from her narrow nose, enhanced by her plump, pouty lips. Lips that turned into a radiant smile when she spun around and pointed excitedly at one of the pictures. As she caught his eyes, still fixed in a glare, her beautiful pearly-white teeth disappeared behind a pout.

He could have sworn she tsk'ed before she turned back to the photographs.

"Did you just tsk, me?"

Venita ignored the deep voice that growled from across the room. *Gmphf, let him see how it feels to be ignored.*

"Woman, I asked you a question."

She turned slowly, allowing her eyes to meet his, and lifted her eyebrows questioningly.

"Are you talking to me? I mean - I seem to have been invisible from the moment I arrived. I really don't want you to extend yourself in any way."

His jaw turned rigid and Venita bit the inside of her cheek to keep the grin back. Jack dropped his chin to his chest, shaking his head. Dax spun his head back to Michael.

"*This* is who you want to pose as my fiancée? An empty headed bimbo? Are you fucking crazy? Anyone who knows me would see right through her. I wouldn't marry someone like her."

His snide remark incited Venita's temper, but Jack reached her in a flash, placing his hand on her elbow warning her to calm down. Glaring at him, she elected to clamp her mouth shut, while her eyes conveyed the message that she was getting out of there.

"Venita," he rasped warningly.

"You heard the...chauvinistic pig. I am out of here. I warned the two of you that a self-absorbed pretty boy like him wouldn't have the sense of a pig in a maze."

She watched him puff up like a blowfish. His ice blue eyes spat shards of glass at her. Baiting him, she idly ran her eyes over the rock-hard muscular contours of his body. He was the embodiment of chiseled perfection. Every aspect of his face looked like it had been shaped by an artist. Perfectly curved eyebrows slanted above his long, black lash-lined eyes that angled down into his straight aquiline nose.

The perfection of his face was capped off with a mouth that left her salivating. *Man...what I would not give to taste those lips.* His top lip had a perfect curve to accent a sexy, full lower lip. A man's mouth made for kissing. A neat scruffy beard enhanced his square jaw. He was very tall, far over six feet and she felt like a little girl next to him, even in her five-inch heels. His dark blond hair was styled in a short spiky cut that gave him a bad boy look.

"Get this useless female out of my sight." He growled through clenched lips.

"Don't bother...I'm gone. Good luck solving your problem, pretty boy."

Venita spun around and strode toward the front door, her hands clasped in tight fists. Jack sprinted after her and cursed when she slammed the door behind her, catching him square on his nose. She turned back around and blasted the door open to hit him on his forehead as he bent forward from the initial abuse to his face.

"Oh shit! I'm sorry...what were you doing...ooh...hahaha...Jeez Jack, you...hahaha..."

Jack stretched to his full intimidating height and glared down at Venita, who tried her best to stop laughing. The moment she looked into his face, she began her fit of laughter again.

"I'm glad you find breaking my damn nose so amusing, Venita."

"Argh, please. Your nose is not broken. Here, let me see."

Jack caught her hand in his and scowled. "Don't you dare touch me. Stop it. I told you...to stay away from me, Vee. Look, let's just all relax for a moment."

She sighed, planted her hands on her hips and looked at him. He was clearly annoyed, even though he looked quite funny with a swollen nose and a red lump on his forehead.

A quirky smile played around her mouth again, but she forced it back when Jack blasted her with his *'I am losing my patience'* look. Throwing her hands in the air, she flashed a disdainful look at a grouchy Dax Kaplan. An unladylike snort sounded from her nose as she gracefully took the three steps into the sunken den to sit down onto one of the plush couches.

Dax's eyes narrowed. In addition to being a sexy siren in fuck-me heels, she was also graceful, confident and classy. Probably just some wannabe actress. *Shit, I do not need this right now.*

The three men had no recourse but to follow her into the den. Venita crossed her legs and leaned back, her hands resting loosely on her lap.

"Dax, you know as well as I do that we need to take a stand against whoever is making those threats. They aren't just targeting you anymore, so we can't keep on ignoring it. You agreed that we would try to draw the person out."

"And the brilliant plan you two came up with was to saddle me with an...undercover fiancée? In case you forgot, Michael, I already have a fiancée."

"Yes, one that nobody has seen, meaning people have no clue what she looks like. You kept the engagement within the family specifically to protect Brooke while she was in Russia. The press knows you are engaged, but not to whom."

"So you want to use...*her* as bait to draw out this extortionist? What exactly is her role going to be?"

"Venita will be your...bodyguard."

Dax did not react at all. His expression did not change, his eyes did not flash. He just watched Michael, waiting. Michael sighed and ran his hands through his hair.

"That's it. She'll be the closest to you and will be there to protect you day and night."

"*She'll* protect *me*?" Initially he chuckled, and then he laughed out right. "How and with what? By throwing those ridiculous heels of hers at the bad guys? *After* they've laughed their heads off?"

Venita ignored him. She did not even look in his direction.

"Dax, if we want to draw them out, we can't have a full team on you the entire time. Your mother is driving me up the wall complaining about having a constant shadow. Do you really want to have this on your back once you and Brooke are married?"

Dax knew that Michael was on the right track. The threats he had received over the past four months had become increasingly violent. Most recently, his parents, brother and friends had been included in the threats. Following an article announcing his engagement, the extortionist threatened Brooke as well. As one of the wealthiest families in the United States, their name was well known, so extortion was not new to them. However, this was the first time that violence was the focus of the threats.

"Very well. But find someone else. I don't want her around me 24/7."

"It's too late to find someone else, Dax. You have to leave in less than two hours. Besides, from what I remember, Venita resembles Brooke closely enough to pass for your fiancée in case someone has seen her before," Jack chipped in.

"She's nowhere close to Brooke. For one thing, Brooke is much taller and curvier. She has shorter hair, plus she's blond. What good is having a little thing like her protecting me? Where did you find her, in the lost and found box at the discarded actresses theater?"

By this time, Venita had heard enough. She slowly rose from the couch and looked at Jack, her voice was husky and laced with anger.

"You can tell this asshole to stick his head where the sun doesn't shine. I wouldn't play his bloody fiancée if he were my last chance to escape a swarm of bees. Hell, I'd rather take my chance with them."

With a flip of her hair, she headed toward the door. Jack sighed and scowled at Dax. They had been friends since high school, but he had never seen him act like such an ass.

"Jesus Dax, what the hell is the matter with you? We're trying to help you and you're acting like a fucking ass."

"Jack, look at her. She is nothing more than an opportunist. You gave her the key to richness."

"Maybe once in a while you should listen when we talk to you, dickhead," Jack snarled furiously. "Venita Baxter is my partner and one of the best fucking trackers I have ever come across. She has a Coral belt in Brazilian jiu-jitsu and I have yet to see her back down from a challenge, no matter how big or strong her opponent is."

Jack got up and began to pace in front of the steps that led into the den.

"Since when do you judge a book by its cover, Dax? You disregarded her the moment she walked through the door. What is really the problem?"

"How old is she?"

"Twenty-nine. Ahh...I see."

Dax's eyes narrowed. "What do you see?" He noticed the flash in Jack's eyes and cursed. "*Hell no!* I just don't have the patience to deal with a stranger around me all the time, Jack, especially not one who will totter and primp all day."

"Yeah, right. What would your reaction have been if she arrived in jeans, a tee shirt and boots? She's playing a part, Dax, with the very same look as the girls you typically have on your arm. You know this is the best opportunity we're going to get. The Cadillac Championship came at the right time."

In addition to running Kaplan Technologies Inc., Dax was also the current World Golf Champion and preparing to defend his title in Miami at the WGC-Cadillac Championship. This year, the purse is $10 million.

Dax nodded, but frowned. He looked from Michael to Jack. "What if that's what this is all about? The championship? This will be the sixth time I claim the title. Maybe someone feels like it's time for me to...step down."

"That was our thought too, which is why having Venita as your fiancée makes sense. Michael and Steven will be around the whole time, except at night."

Dax looked as if he were about to choke. "At

night...you mean I have to..."

"Yes, Dax. No one would ever believe you and your fiancée sleep in separate rooms."

Nor would they believe I haven't slept with her at all. Brooke left for Russia the same night they became engaged. He sighed. Their engagement was not a coming together borne of heated love and lust. They had known one another for years, felt comfortable together and had decided they could build a solid marriage. His family and friends were not happy with the engagement, because they were certain that he was not in love with his fiancée.

"Then I trust you got the Gary Player Villa for us."

"We initially did, but changed it to a three bedroom spa suite. One room for each of us and one for you and Venita. Don't you growl at me, Dax. The point is for her to keep an eye on you during the night. You need your sleep if you want to win. Besides, it is not good to tempt fate, and the villa is just too secluded to be safe."

Dax dropped his head in his hands and sighed heavily. No matter how much he hated sharing his life for the next few weeks with that...that sexy, sensual and seriously tempting woman, he knew they were right.

"Fine. Just make sure she knows to stay out

of my personal space when we're alone."

Jack shook his head and went outside, to look for Venita. He found her sitting on the edge of a fountain beside the house, having an animated discussion with two massive silver Great Danes. They sat on their haunches in front of her and their ears twitched as if they were listening attentively to her. His mouth quirked when he heard what she was saying.

"Yes, I quite agree, Lupus. He might be attractive as sin and have a body Hercules would kill for, but he is a bloody jerk. No wonder someone is threatening him."

"Vee." She started and looked up.

"Good, can we leave now? I might still be in time to catch the Yankees."

"You'll have to watch it on the plane."

Venita's eyes narrowed and she glared at Jack. "No. No way in hell. I am *out*."

"Vee, look. All of this is really frustrating and he's got a lot to deal with right now."

"That gives him no right to insult and belittle me. The answer is no, Jack."

"Come on, Vee. I really need you to do this for me. He's one of my best friends. I've known his parents since grade school and his house became my second home."

"No fair, Jack. Aarggh! Okay. On two

conditions," Venita gave in on a sigh.

"Name it."

"I want a real, sincere, heartfelt apology from him and I am *not* dyeing my hair."

"Ah fuck, Venita! Why don't you just ask me to cut off my arm instead?"

Venita shrugged. "I guess that's it then."

Jack cursed and growled low in his throat. He grabbed her hand and dragged her back to the house.

"Easy, partner. Remember the heels I'm wearing."

"Yeah, and I've seen you run in those spikes before, so stop complaining."

He made her wait in the foyer and disappeared into the den. He sighed, first looking at Dax, then at Michael.

"So? Where is she?"

"She has a condition before she agrees."

"Oh, here we go." Dax stretched his legs out in front of him as he leaned back against the couch.

"Zip it, Dax. She has the right to ask for it."

"What does the lady want?"

"She said, and I quote, '*a real, sincere, heartfelt apology*' from you."

Once again, Dax's expression did not change, except for a slight twinkle that appeared in his eyes.

Michael glanced at Jack. *Hmm...interesting.*

"Very well."

"Dax, if you..."

"Yes, Jack. Real, sincere, and heartfelt. I got it."

Jack shook his head and went to fetch Venita. She walked back into the den and stood next to the couch. Waiting. Dax remained in his lazy position and slowly looked her up and down. His cock twitched and he cursed softly. With a heavy sigh, he got up and turned to face her.

"Miss Baxter, it has come to my attention that I have been acting like a...dickhead and may have said certain things out of...context. Please accept my sincere apology for anything I might have said to upset your tender disposition."

"And of course I am too much of an empty headed bimbo to realize that you insulted me again with that sad excuse of an apology. You know, Lupus is right. You are nothing but a pretty boy with no sense of decorum."

"Lupus? My dog...what the hell does my dog have to do with this?"

"Well, at least he has some class and personality. Something his owner is sorely lacking."

Michael and Jack burst out laughing. Dax glowered at Venita. His irritation with her was rising higher with each passing moment. He took a deep breath. *I wonder what Jack would do if I throw his partner off a cliff in Miami?* This was a very real possibility, if this was how she was going to behave as his fiancée.

"Very well. I formed an unfair opinion of you and insulted you. I apologize."

Venita's eyes narrowed, but she knew she was not going to receive anything more from him. She straightened and stared at him.

"Very well. Now, my dearest love, kiss me."

"What?"

"You heard me."

"Vee...what..."

"We are supposed to pretend to be an engaged couple in-love. I need to see how good he is at acting and how much more work I'll have to do to make it believable."

She had turned to Jack to explain and when she spun back to face Dax, he was directly in front of her. With one hand on her waist, he fisted his other hand in her hair, yanking her hard against him. Swooping down, his lips covered hers and he kissed her. On her gasping 'oh', his tongue slipped past her lips and he deepened the kiss immediately. Without realizing it, Venita's hands crept around his back and she leaned into the kiss. Heat flushed through her body, wetting her panties. Her nipples became tightly budded and painfully aroused. *Oh, bloody hell, I am in trouble!*

Michael, clearing his throat loudly, broke them apart and Dax released her slowly, his hand still fisted in her hair. He pulled her head back and looked into her eyes.

"Don't challenge me, woman. You'll lose every time."

She rubbed her hips against his rock hard cock and smiled sensually.

"Really, honey buns?"

She pulled herself from his arms before he could react. With shuttered eyes, he watched her storm toward the door, unable to remember the last time a woman gave him such a hard-on. In a hoarse voice, he turned to Jack and Michael.

"This is a fucking bad idea. That woman is just too..."

"Too what? Cheeky, sassy, assertive? What?"

Dax pressed his lips flat and glared at Jack. Michael chuckled and his assessment hit the nail on the head.

"Too damn hot."

They looked at Dax and Jack frowned. "Are you saying said that you are attracted to Vee?"

"Fuck, Jack...what do you think? You expect me to sleep next to...that...those perfect pert ass and luscious boobs without getting a hard on? I'm a hot blooded man, not a damn eunuch!"

"Hmm...well, Brooke knows that you've been taking care of your sexual needs while she is in Russia, so why is this such an issue?"

"She is your partner, Jack, and if the sparks between you are anything to go by, probably more than that."

"Nope. We've known each other too long and we're just very good friends. But I'll kick your ass if you hurt her."

"Then you better warn her to keep her distance. If she keeps rubbing herself against me and kissing me, she will carry the consequences."

Michael and Jack looked at each other and winked. They had been opposed to Dax marrying Brooke from the moment he told them of the engagement. Granted she was beautiful, clever and oozed class, but she was as cold as the Antarctic. What kind of fiancée would insist that her man have sex with other woman if he has the need? Dax had never wanted for female companionship. Women drooled over him and he made use of them whenever he felt like it.

But, even he frowned at Brooke when she insisted he find sexual relief during her absence. He had always believed that once he made a commitment to someone, then that was it. No more fooling around. In essence, he was a one-woman man. Jack suspected that Dax had his own doubts about a future with Brooke. Maybe he just needed the right woman to give him a little push to make him see the light.

"Well, that might be a tad difficult, Bud. Remember, you have to make the world believe *she* is the woman that captured your heart. If you don't touch and kiss in public, no one will believe you two are head over heels."

Dax ran his hands through his hair and growled.

"This is a fucked up plan the two of you have come up with, you know."

"Come on, Bud. I don't understand the problem. You've never had an issue touching and kissing a beautiful woman let alone letting her touch you. Why now?"

Because she totally captivated him. From the moment she stepped through the door. His heart actually missed a beat when their eyes met, then it started racing. He had to take a deep breath to calm it down. *Mine. She belongs to me.* Those were the thoughts that flashed through his mind - about the same time his cock reacted. He was still as hard as a rock.

His issue with Venita Baxter was that he had never in his life felt such an immediate reaction to a woman. Never. Not once.

"Just bloody warn her. She touches me when we're alone, I *will* fuck her."

Available on your favorite platform:
www.books2read.com/CaughtinBetween

MORE BOOKS BY LINZI BASSET

Club Devil's Cove Series
His Devil's Desire – Book 1
His Devil's Heat – Book 2
His Devil's Wish – Book 3
His Devil's Mercy – Book 4
His Devil's Chain – Book 5

Club Wicked Cove Series
Desperation: Ceejay's Absolution–Book 1
Desperation: Colt's Acquittal – Book 2
Exploration: Nolan's Regret – Book 3
Merciful: Seth's Revenge – Book 4
Claimed: Parnell's Gift – Book 5
Decadent: Kent's Desire – Book 6

Club Alpha Cove Series
His FBI Sub – Book 1
His Ice Baby Sub – Book 2
His Vanilla Sub – Book 3
His Fiery Sub – Book 4
His Sassy Sub – Book 5
Their Bold Sub – Book 6
His Brazen Sub – Book 7
His Defiant Sub – Book 8
His Forever Sub – Book 9
His Cherished Sub – Book 10

Claimed Bride

For Amy – Their Beloved Sub – Book 11

Their Sub Novella Series
No Option – Book 1
Done For – Book 2
For This – Book 3
Their Sub Series Boxset

Their Command Series
Say Yes – Book 1
Say Please – Book 2
Say Now – Book 3
Their Command Series Boxset

Paranormal Books
The Flame Dragon King - Metallic Dragons #1
Slade: The First Touch
Azriel: Angel of Destruction

Romance Suspense

The Bride Series
Claimed Bride – Book 1

Caught Series
Caught in Between – Book 1
Caught in His Web – Book 2

Linzi Basset

The Tycoon Series
The Tycoon and His Honey Pot – Book 1
The Tycoon's Blondie – Book 2
The Tycoon's Mechanic – Book 3

Standalone Titles
Her Prada Cowboy
Never Leave Me, Baby
Now is Our Time
The Wildcat that Tamed the Tycoon
The Poet's Lover
Sarah: The Life of Me

Naughty Christmas Story
Her Santa Dom

Boxset
A Santa to Love

Books Co-Written as Isabel James

The White Pearl Series
Double Shot Espresso – Book 1
The Crow's Nest – Book 2
The White Pearl Boxset

Christmas Novella
Santa's Kiss

Claimed Bride

Boxset
A Santa to Love

**Poetry Bundle by Linzi Basset & James
Calderaro**

Love Unbound - Poems of the Heart

ABOUT THE AUTHOR

"Isn't it a universal truth that it's our singular experiences and passion, for whatever thing or things, which molds us all into the individuals we become? Whether it's hidden in the depths of our soul or exposed for all to see?"

Linzi Basset is a South African born animal rights supporter with a poet's heart, and she is also a bestselling fiction writer of suspense filled romance erotica books; who as the latter, refuses to be bound to any one sub-genre. She prefers instead to stretch herself as a storyteller which has resulted in her researching and writing historical and even paranormal themed works.

Her initial offering: Club Alpha Cove, a BDSM club suspense series released back in 2015, reached Amazon's Bestseller list, and she has been on those lists ever since. Labelling her as prolific is a gross understatement as just a few short years later she has now been published thirty-nine times; a total which fails to take into account the three other published works of her alter ego: Isabel James who co-authors—nor does it include the five additional new works marked for imminent release.

"I write from the inside out. My stories are both inside me and a part of me so it can be either pleasurable to release them or painful to carve them out. I live every moment of every story I write. So, if you're looking for spicy and suspenseful, I'm your girl . . . woman . . . writer . . . you know what I mean!"

Linzi believes that by telling stories in her own voice, she can better share with her readers the essence of her being: her passionate nature; her motivations; and her wildest fantasies. She feels every touch as she writes, every kiss, every harsh word uttered, and this to her is the key to a never-ending love of writing.

Ultimately, all books by Linzi Basset are about passion. To her, passion is the driving force of all emotion; whether it be lust, desire, hate, trust, or love. This is the underlying message contained in her books. Her advice: "Believe in the passions driving your desires; live them; enjoy them; and allow them to bring you happiness."

STALK ME

If you'd like to look me up, please follow any of these links.

While you're enjoying some of my articles, interviews and poems on my website, www.linzibassetauthor.com why not subscribe to my Newsletter and be the first to know about new releases and win free books.

Twitter: http://bit.ly/2wjRgc8 and Isabel James: http://bit.ly/2xZXShM
On facebook: Friend me on: http://bit.ly/2gJZyYV or Isabel James on: http://bit.ly/2vPeS90
Like me on: http://bit.ly/2wSmpI9 and Isabel James: http://bit.ly/2xfHrQN
Website: www.linzibassetauthor.com And http://linzibasset.wixsite.com/isabeljames
Follow me on Amazon: http://amzn.to/2wS2dpS and UK - http://amzn.to/2ePQlK9 and
Isabel James: http://amzn.to/2wAmGN9
Follow me on Goodreads: http://bit.ly/2vZw6EP
All Author-Page: http://bit.ly/2wUxYxF and Isabel James: http://bit.ly/2wUy7Bd

Bookbub: http://bit.ly/2wUwIZG
Radish Fiction: http://bit.ly/2zEK3pW

Like my Facebook pages:
Linzi's Poetry Page: http://bit.ly/2wS5EfY
Club Wicked Cove: http://bit.ly/2wUyjQX
Club Alpha Cove: http://bit.ly/2xfEZtE
AND, don't forget to join Linzi's Lair for loads of fun!
http://bit.ly/2wUfzks

Don't be shy, pay me a visit, anytime!

Printed in Poland
by Amazon Fulfillment
Poland Sp. z o.o., Wrocław